BOOTHILL BRAND

Also available in Large Print
by Lee Floren:

Ride the Wild Country

Lee Floren

BOOTHILL BRAND

Parents Are Responsible for
Child's Book Choices

CALHOUN COUNTY PUBLIC LIBRARY SYSTEM
200 N. Pear Street
Blountstown, Florida 32424
904 / 674-8773

G.K.HALL &CO.
Boston, Massachusetts
1990

Copyright © MCMLXXIX by Lee Floren.

All rights reserved.

Published in Large Print by arrangement with
Leisure Books, a division of Dorchester Publishing Co.

G.K. Hall Large Print Book Series.

Set in 16 pt Plantin.

Library of Congress Cataloging in Publication Data

Floren, Lee.
    Boothill brand / Lee Floren.
       p. cm.—(G.K. Hall large print book series) (Nightingale series)
   ISBN 0-8161-4968-2 (lg. print)
   1. Large type books. I. Title.
[PS3511.L697B6   1990]
813'.54—dc20   90-32430

I

RIC WILLIAMS was playing cards with three of his farmers when he heard the loud and angry voices out on Black Butte's rainswept Main Street that afternoon on May fifteenth, 1899.

Whist game forgotten, Ric got hurriedly up from his chair. "Somebody's arguing out on Main Street!"

His farmers also had risen. They were in Ric's living-quarters tied onto the back of his land-locator's office. They hurried across the office to peer out the two windows looking out on Black Butte's two-block long Main Street.

"Looks like trouble ahead," one farmer said.

"You said it, Mullins." Ric spoke slowly, heart hammering.

He'd located homesteaders as a Federal Land agent for a year on this grass and sooner or later he'd figured hell would break loose between his few homesteaders and this country's last remaining big cow-outfit—Greg Mattson's Half Circle V.

And now that trouble had arrived. . . .

Two men stood across the muddy street on the plank sidewalk in front of Victor's barber-shop. Despite the rain their voices carried clearly. Their loud voices had brought almost all Black Butte's citizens out, Ric saw.

For Black Butte was celebrating. This was Founders Day. For thirty odd years ago his father—now dead Brent Williams—and Greg Mattson's father, also gone forever, had driven thousands of wild Texas longhorns onto Black Butte's tall buffalo grass—and had started the town of Black Butte.

Streamers hung across the mud from false-front to false-front. This celebration also was in honor of the rain which had fallen steadily for over a week—the first real rain on this grass in two long dry years.

"The one in the yeller slicker is Jim Young," one farmer said.

Ric said, "Right you are, Griffin."

"Sure hope he don't pack a gun," the third farmer said, " 'cause everybody's seen how fast Kid Hannigan can handle his pistol."

"I hope so, too, Hess," Ric said.

This was the last day of the three day celebration. This forenoon there'd been a shooting contest.

Cans had been saved for months for the competition. Three guns had come out in the finals. One gun had belonged to Greg Mattson, one to Ric Williams—and the other to Kid Hannigan.

Each six-shooter had held five bullets. Each gun had had three tries. Greg Mattson and Ric had scored fourteen out of fifteen to tie for second. Kid Hannigan had hit with all fifteen bullets.

Ric and his farmers went outside to stand under the wooden awning hanging over Ric's office.

Ric heard Kid Hannigan say, "After this watch where you're walkin', sodbuster! You damn' hoemen don't need the whole damn' sidewalk!"

The gunman had emphasized the words *hoemen* and *sodbuster*. Since barbwire and windmills had started invading central Montana's once-free-and-open cowrange the two words had become more of an insult than *sonofabitch*.

Ric said slowly, "I better get over there.

Jim might have a pistol on him and might be foolish enough to try to use it."

"He tol' me he was three years on the Detroit police force afore he come out here," Mullins said, "so he might be able to use a short-gun good."

Ric said, "He's got a wife and two little girls back in Detroit. And I guess they're waiting to come here to live with daddy—and this they can't do if daddy gets in a gun-trap and gets killed."

"You said it, Ric," Hess said.

Ric stepped into the mud. "You boys stay here. You're all bachelors but stay out, please."

Hess and Mullins and Griffin stayed behind. Until the coming of Jim Young those three were the only farmers Ric had located on homesteads, and the three had arrived last August, too late for planting.

The past winter had been terrible. Some claimed it was worse that the winter-kill winter of '86-'87, if that were possible. Nevertheless, the three farmers had managed to somehow live it out on a diet of jackrabbits, cottontails, a razor-thin deer. By now the buffalo was gone. Uncle Sam's sharpshooters had seen to that.

Mud sloshed around Ric's boots. He

hadn't had time to get into his slicker. He was sopping wet by the middle of the street.

Kid Hannigan's boss—Greg Mattson—stood with his back against the barbershop, big and wide-shouldered in his dark-colored raincoat. Two of his Half Circle V riders stood on his right, another two on his left.

"Here comes the land locator," Mattson told Kid Hannnigan.

Hannigan said, "Keep an eye on him," and didn't even look at the advancing Ric Williams.

"I'll do that," Greg Mattson said.

Mattson turned his dull gray eyes on Ric. He and Ric were the same age. They were the only get of two Texas cowmen who had trailed longhorns into this area—two men who had died within the last few years, as firm in friendship as the day they'd tumbled the first Texas cow onto this high grass.

But not so their sons. . . .

Nobody knew why but Greg Mattson and Richard Williams had apparently hated each other the first moment their eyes had been laid on the other. Both had gone to grammar school here in Black Butte.

They had fought fistfight after fistfight

through all eight grades. They had fought over nothing. They had fought just to be fighting.

Most of the fistfights had been ties. Both boys had fought until they could no longer raise their arms. They then rested briefly and fought again.

Old Brent Williams and Scott Mattson had more than once talked this over. First, both had decided to thrash their sons. This they had then done, but two weeks later their sons were at it again.

The two cowmen had given up.

Now Greg Mattson's gray eyes met Ric Williams' blue eyes. Hate and contempt lay in the young cowman's eyes plainly visible.

Ric stepped up onto the planks. He spoke to Jim Young. "What seems to be the trouble here?"

Greg Mattson answered for the farmer. "None of your damn' business, Williams."

Ric said pointedly, "I spoke to Young, remember?"

"An' I answered," Mattson said.

Jim Young looked at Mattson. "I can answer my own questions, cattle-king! I don't need your help!"

Greg Mattson laughed. His cowpunchers made snickering sounds. With difficulty, Ric

Williams overlooked this. He looked at Jim Young.

Young was one of those men who retained their youth longer than others. Despite being married and father of two he looked like a boy of eighteen or thereabouts.

He was unsteady in his high-laced boots. Plainly, he'd been drinking—but drinking was nothing new on Founders Day here in Black Butte town.

Rumor had that on this day even the town preacher got peacefully and blissfully drunk in the church. His wife got drunk in public along with others of the town's leading female citizens.

Young spoke to Ric. "I'm over twenty-one."

Ric nodded. "I grant that. But you sure aren't sober."

"Sober as I ever will be."

All drunks more or less made the same statement, Ric knew, so he tactfully changed the subject. "What happened?"

"Hannigan here deliberately crossed the sidewalk to shoulder me," Jim Young said.

Kid Hannigan snorted. "Damn' farmer's lyin', land-locator. He was so pie-eyed he staggered into me an' almost knocked me into the mud!"

"My man's right," Greg Mattson hurriedly said.

Ric Williams again disregarded his old-time enemy. "Come with me, Young," he said.

"Why?" Mattson asked.

Ric said to Mattson, "I wasn't talking to you, Greg. Why don't you at least act a little civilized and speak only when spoken to, like your father told you when you were a kid?"

Ric heard a few women titter at this, but the watching men remained silent, only the sound of the rain being heard. A glance across the street showed his three farmers standing where he'd left them.

Mattson said hotly, "Another one like that, Williams, an' you an' me tangle again, savvy?"

Kid Hannigan spoke to Ric. "This is between me an' this farmer, land-locator. Not between me an' you. He bumped me, not you."

Ric looked at Kid Hannigan. Short, bearded, blue-eyed, muscular, legs bowed from the barrel of a horse. Typical drifter, a drifting gunman. Hannigan had come onto this range last year about the same time Ric's three farmers had shown up and staked out homestead claims northeast six miles on Hell Creek.

Greg Mattson had immediately hired the man. And not to punch cattle, some said—definitely not as a cowpuncher.

Rumors floated around the tough personage of Kid Hannigan. Some claimed he fled north out of Wyoming after a rustler-cowman war. Others said he was a Texas renegade wanted by the Rangers in the Lone Star State.

Ric said slowly, "Everybody's celebrating, Kid. A little drunk, most of us—so why not blame it on the booze and the celebration and let it go at that?"

A woman said, "Amen to that, Ric."

Ric looked at the woman. She was almost as wide as tall. Her strong body wore bib overalls and a blue cotton shirt. High heeled cowpuncher boots encased her big feet.

His eyes traveled to the young woman standing beside Kitty O'Neill, longtime owner of Black Butte's only saloon. This woman had been in town only a week or so.

This woman stood about five feet four and had blonde hair. Ric judged her about his age, or a year or two younger. Her name was Melissa Wentworth and she dealt poker in Kitty's saloon.

She was Black Butte's first lady gambler. Ric had been coming out of the post office the day she'd stepped down from the northbound stage that ran north into Timber Mountain, Saskatchewan, Canada, some forty miles away.

He stopped and stared like a country bumpkin. She'd seen his awkward gawkiness and then had looked away, plainly amused.

She'd then walked, suitcase in hand, upstreet toward the saloon. Ric had returned to his office.

He'd dreamed of her that night.

Now her deep green eyes seemed to tease him. He said to Kitty O'Neill. "You said a big mouthful, Kitty."

"I sent Sonny Horner for Ike Ratchford," the saloon-keeper said. "That lazy fat old sheriff should soon be putting in his appearance." She spoke with a bit of Old Sod brogue.

"Here comes the sheriff now," somebody said.

Kitty O'Neill said, "And on the double, too. And he don't look too drunk, either—settin' aroun' the office in Jones' barn playin' pinochle with those other ol' bats."

Kitty had come in behind Mattson-Williams Longhorns. The young man who now was a middle-aged man named Ike Ratchford had been Black Butte's law for thirty years, too.

For almost thirty years the female saloonkeeper and the man who'd become Black Butte's first and only star-toter had kept up a running banter, but let somebody say something bad about Sheriff Ike—or, for that matter, about Kitty O'Neill in the lawman's presence—and hell was soon to break loose.

Ric felt relief touch him at the sight of Sheriff Ratchford's figure barging toward him. Ratchford had bounced him on his knee when he'd been a mere boy. For that matter, he'd done likewise to young Greg Mattson, too.

Ratchford read the problem at a glance. He rudely shoved his big body between Jim Young and Kid Hannigan. Anger flushed Hannigan's beefy face, but he made no objections.

Ric wondered why until he glanced at Greg Mattson and saw Mattson nod slightly.

"No fightin' here," the sheriff said shortly. "This is a day of celebration, not of fightin'. Greg, you watch this gunman of yours, savvy?"

"Gunman?" Greg Mattson said.

"That's what I call him," the sheriff answered shortly. He spoke to Kid Hannigan. "You get your hand on thet gun in my town, mister, an' you go to one of two places—my jail or the morgue!"

"Who says so?" Kid Hannigan demanded.

"I do, mister. An' don't forgit it, either."

Ric noticed Hannigan discreetly kept his hand away from his holstered pistol. He remembered Kid Hannigan's fast gun and deadly accuracy. He also knew that if Hannigan started anything in this town Ike Ratchford would arrest him, even though it might cost the old lawman his life.

Ratchford was a man of his word.

"You talk awful rough, Ike," Greg Mattson said.

Ratchford clipped, "I've said enough. Now clear the street, all of you."

Kitty O'Neill said, "Get movin' all of us."

Ric Williams now breathed normally.

Greg Mattson said to Ric, "You deliberately settled this new farmer on my back Sage Crick grass an' water, Williams."

"He didn't settle me there," Jim Young hurriedly corrected. "I picked out that one hundred an' sixty acres myself on his big wall map."

Ike Ratchford said, "Did you hear me? I tol' all of you to clear the street."

Townspeople began leaving. Greg Mattson looked at Ric and than said to Kid Hannigan, "There'll be another time, Kid."

"There always is," Kid Hannigan said.

Mattson and his hired gun turned and went toward Kitty O'Neill's saloon, the other Half Circle V hands following. Ric's three farmers then crossed the street.

Ric spoke to Young, "You'd better stay close to us others, Jim. Or go home, but not alone, understand?"

"Ambush?"

Ric shrugged. "Not from Greg Mattson. He's the son of an old cowman and so far as I've known he's always played fair and above the table—but that Kid Hannigan rat. . . ."

Young nodded. "I understand."

Ric looked at the three other farmers. They sported sour, down-cast faces. They had told him they were all three ex-cowpunchers who'd tired of rodding the other man's dogies at a mere two bucks and found a month.

"I'll stick with you boys," Young said.

"I'd admire a slug of red-eye for my cold belly," Jake Mullins said. Mullins was a stocky man of around thirty. His nose had once been broken and had been set a little crooked. "But the only saloon is Kitty's an' I don't want no trouble with them Mattson men. I've had too much trouble in my life so far without lookin' for more." He added, "But let it come an' I ain't runnin'."

"Same for me," George Hess said.

Ward Griffin said, "Me, too."

"Ratchford's going into the saloon," Ric said, "and Greg Mattson has known Kitty ever since he can remember—and he'll respect her place. He won't let his hands start trouble in Kitty's."

George Hess said slowly, "So what's holdin' us back, men?"

"Nothing that I can see," Ric assured.

They started up-street. Kitty and Melissa were just entering the saloon. Kitty's raincoat fitted her square body like a tablecloth had been thrown over her but Melissa's raincoat hugged her small waist like it had been glued to her hips.

Ric liked what he saw.

Suddenly, he noticed a young woman standing out of the rain in the Mercantile's front. The woman had noticed Ric's admiring glance.

Her lips showed a small, amused smile. She was small—not over five feet—and young and pretty—a wholesome prettiness that came from rain and sun and this endless land.

Her eyes met Ric's. She then looked aside, still smiling. Ric felt irritation.

Her name was Martha Stewart. She'd been born and reared in Black Butte, her father having for years been the town's only schoolteacher.

Malcolm Stewart had resigned his teaching job last spring. Next year Martha would preside over the town's school children. She had just been graduated from the state normal school.

She and Ric and Greg Mattson had gone to grammar school together. She'd gone to Malta for high school, as had Ric—but Greg Mattson had quit school after the eighth grade to work on big Half Circle V.

Martha tossed her head, wheeled, and entered the Merc. She too showed a small waist and nice hips, Ric noticed.

Stocky George Hess had caught the play. "She's mad an' she's after you, Ric," he said.

Ric only smiled.

II

Rain still fell when the Black Butte rodeo-finals began at one that same afternoon. Malcolm Stewart and Ric were judges in the women's relay race.

Three women riders had made the finals. One was Martha Stewart, another was Jennie Queen, a town girl, and the third was none other than blonde Melissa Wentworth, gambler.

Each woman rode four horses. Each horse ran a quarter mile. When the horse had finished his lap his rider left him on the dead run, taking the saddle with her.

She then ran to her next mount, held by her handler. Up went the saddle, the cinch was caught, slipped into tackaberry buckle —and the rider swung up, the end of the latigo in hand, the cinch being tightened on the dead run.

And a horse ground out another lap, ears back and tail floating in his speed.

Martha and Melissa were neck-to-neck on

the fourth and last horse, Jennie Queen a pace behind. Ric was surprised to see Melissa—whom he'd considered a town woman—handle a horse and saddle with such lightning ease.

Martha and her four running-horses had won the women's relay race for a number of years, now—but this time the young schoolteacher had plenty of competition.

Schoolteacher Malcolm Stewart looked at his stop-watch. "They're grinding it out in record time, Ric."

"Miss Wentworth surprises me," Ric said.

Stewart smiled softly. "You're young yet, Ric. When you get to my advanced age what a woman does—or can do—will fail to surprise you."

Ric glanced at the schoolteacher. This man had caned him and held him after school for fighting with Greg Mattson but yet he admired and respected the thin, gray-haired man very much.

He knew Greg Mattson held the same feelings toward this sagebrush scholar, as did the entire range and town of Black Butte.

"Advanced age?" Ric joked. "Dad said you were only twenty when he and Scott Mattson picked you out of cowpuncher ranks and said you'd have to be the local schoolteacher. That'd make you around fifty, old man Stewart."

"Right you are. There they slant the near curve. This mud—Makes for slippery riding. Jennie is gaining."

Malcolm Stewart was correct. Jennie Queen's last horse—a big sorrel—was fast and sure-footed, shod all around. He'd eaten up the distance and when the three horses stretched out for the far stretch his head was pounding the flank of Melissa Wentworth's bay gelding.

Melissa rode Mattson Half Circle V horses. She'd not had much time to practice but apparently she'd soon learned the speed and ability of her broncs, for she handled them like a veteran.

"Jennie's pulling up," Malcolm Stewart said, again glancing at his watch. "That sorrel she's on is a tough horse. I'm just praying that none slide in the mud on that far turn."

"Lot of mud there," Ric said.

Ric glanced at the grandstand. It was a roar of color and cheers. Each had his favorite woman rider. Each let the world know about it in loud hollering and wild gestures.

Ric's blood thrilled. Nothing like a good horserace to make a man stand on stirrups, he thought. No wonder it's called the Sport of Kings. He held his breath as the three lunging Montana horses began the last quarter-circle before heading into the homestretch.

Now the three running horses were on the stretch's outermost point. His breath caught. Jennie's sorrel made a slight slip. For a moment Ric thought the horse would lose his footing and go down.

But the horse held his footing. He ran on gamely, but the losing of his stride might cost him the race—and besides, the town-girl rode on the outer edge.

Martha's horse held the rail. Melissa's bronc was between Martha and Jennie.

The girls made the bend and their horses came in on the final stretch, Martha's horse a half-head in the lead, Melissa's Half Circle V horse a pace behind, with the big sorrel of Jennie Queen closing in slowly, running his loyal heart out.

"By gosh, that sorrel might do it," Malcolm Stewart said. "This will set a new stampede record, Ric."

"It'll be a hard one to judge if they finish like this," Ric said.

"Take a lawyer to make the decision, Ric, and you're one. I should never have been picked to judge this, seeing my daughter's in it. I hereby and now appoint you sole judge, thus eliminating myself."

Ric Williams grinned boyishly. "Thanks," he said.

He spurred over to the finish tape. The three running-horses came in a bunch. The tape broke and the three thundered past, riders beginning to pull in.

Ric spoke to the schoolteacher. "Miss Wentworth by a horse's whisker," he said.

Malcolm Stewart nodded. "Appeared that way to me."

"Jennie and Martha a tie for second," Ric said.

"I go with that, too." Again the thin teacher looked at his watch. "Record time, Ric."

The announcer rode up, megaphone in hand. "Results, judges?" Ric told him. The three women sat their horses in a bunch, waiting. The announcer spieled off the names of Martha and Jennie. "And the winner in a new record time, Miss Melissa Wentworth!"

Ric noticed the cheering for Melissa was not its normal length and loudness. He understood. A stranger had ridden in and captured the prize that up until now had always been won by a home-town girl. These people were very clannish and always backed another townsperson.

That was only normal. Most had been in Black Butte for years. Some had been born here and spent their lives here.

Malcolm Stewart was rodeo-manager, a position he'd held for years because of his high social standing as the town's only teacher. He and Melissa loped around the arena with Jennie and Martha riding behind.

Ric did not make the triumphal tour. He and Malcolm Stewart would team-rope next. They'd have tough competition in Greg Mattson and Kid Hannigan. George Hess and Ward Griffin, two of the farmers, had also made the team-roping finals, Hess roping heads and Griffin the hind legs.

Hess and Griffin were fast and sure ropers, too. They each roped three calves, working against the stop-watching. When it came to the last calf the farmers were ahead by a few seconds and Half Circle V and Ric and Stewart almost in a tie, Mattson and Kid Hannigan a flick ahead.

Ric coiled his wet catch-rope. With the schoolteacher in this event the announcer—

fat Mike Weldon—was timer and judge. Ric tossed his kinky, stiff lariat to a tender.

"Something new, Henry."

The tender tossed up a new maguey rope. Ric shook his head and tossed it back. "No soapweed. I can't handle that as well as manila."

This time he received a thirty-five foot manila lasso. He shook out a loop, especially noticing how easily the rope ran through the hondo. "This'll do," he said.

Melissa Wentworth pulled her horse in close to his. Ric looked at her blonde loveliness and said, "Congratulations."

White teeth showed. Green eyes were full of life. "Thank you, kind sir."

Ric glanced at Martha Stewart who sat her saddle between him and her father. Maybe he was wrong, but he was sure that when he'd looked at Martha she'd been watching him and Melissa, but now she was apparently seriously engaged in conversation with her father.

Ric hid his smile.

Naturally he'd escorted Martha to various social functions such as local country dances. So, for that matter, had Greg Mattson. Such was only logical. Eligible and single women were scarce here on the frontier. Both had also at one time or other gone to such with Jennie Queen, one of the few other girls in Black Butte.

Jennie's father owned the Mercantile, Black Butte's only community store. Ric's father had started the emporium a few months after arriving in this area with Scott Mattson and their wild Texas longhorns.

But running a ranch and a store had been too much and within five years he'd sold the Merc to Jennie's family.

"You've ridden relay before, I take it?" Ric asked.

Melissa shook her head. "First time, Ric. I practiced on the sly since coming here. Greg asked me to represent Half Circle V so I promised, not even guessing at what I was entering."

Ric had liked her calling him Ric instead of the usual Mr. Williams. But when she called Greg Mattson by his first name with such familiarity he soured somewhat.

"You ride good," he said.

"Thank you. And you rope and ride broncos in a first-class manner."

"Tough competition, Miss Wentworth."

Miss Wentworth scowled slightly. "I like Black Butte. It makes me feel at home. I guess it's because I was raised in a small

Nebraska town. But as long as I'm here, why not call me Melissa?"

"Melissa it is, then."

She smiled. "You know what Melissa means?"

"You can't stump me. Greek One, Doc Myers the teacher—Montana U. Means honey."

"Yes, and means a bee, too."

Ric tried something. "Have you a stinger like a bee?" He realized instantly he'd overstepped. Her face told him that. The irritation caused by the Jim Young—Kid Hannigan ruckus was still on him. It colored his thoughts with its danger and lay always in the background. "Forget it," he said shortly.

She looked at him. "Forget what?"

"I went too far. Sometimes a joke—if that could be called such—blows up in one's face. Well, time Malcolm and I rope."

He and Malcolm Stewart reined their horses in on each side of the rope barrier, loops built, both tied hard-and-fast to saddlehorns. When the calf came roaring from the chute he'd hit the barrier, knock the rope down, and then he was their game.

Ric glanced at the chute. A big husky

longhorn calf wrestled with himself in the barrier, tail up and ready to go.

The rodeo-manager said, "All set, ropers?"

Ric nodded. Malcolm Stewart nodded.

"Turn him loose, boys."

The chute gate opened. The calf hesitated not a moment. He leaped out, tail up, hoofs hammering. He hit the barrier. It went down. Two roping horses leaped forward.

Shod hoofs threw back mud. The schoolteacher's loop sang out, hung in front of the calf's head, came back, settled, caught. Ric's loop went singing out, flat, the calf's hind legs went into it—but Ric was slower than usual, and he knew it.

His whole attention hadn't been on his rope. Kid Hannigan and Jim Young's troubles lay in the background. The calf went down, roping horses pulled him out flat, and the announcer bawled out the roping-time.

Flankers came out, loosened ropes. Stewart and Ric coiled lassos. Stewart said, "Slow time," and let it go at that. All in the game, Ric thought.

Greg Mattson and Kid Hannigan roped next. Their combined time was less than that of Ric and Stewart. Then came the farmers. Hess and Griffin. They roped with hard sureness.

It was beautiful to watch. Ric guessed both were Texas men. Down in Texas you had to lay out your loop fast and sure. That was brush country. You ran your stock into a small clearing. You had to catch there or maybe—so never get another chance again.

He tried to remember back. Had either of these two farmers ever told where they'd come from? Here in Montana you asked few questions, if any. Many Montanas were wanted men in other states. They'd come to the raw wilderness to lose their identity and be safe from the law. Most of the waddies who'd come up hazing Texas cattle were wanted men down south.

A few inquisitive souls had asked questions. They'd received answers in the form of bullets.

The farmers won. Half Circle V was second. Ric and Stewart were third. Stewart said, "Well, we got in the money, anyway." Ric was sure his voice held short disappointment.

"My fault," Ric said.

Stewart had no answer.

They rode to the paymaster and collected third money when, in Ric's estimation, they should have had first, as usual. They split the fifty dollars two ways and considered themselves lucky.

Greg Mattson and Kid Hannigan rode past. Neither glanced at Ric or said hello.

The three of them—Mattson, Hannigan, and Ric—were in the saddle-bronc riding finals. Usually this was a bitter contest between Greg Mattson and Ric but now a new figure was in it—the shadow of squat, gun-throwing Kid Hannigan, bearded and swaggering and tough.

The Williams Bar Diamond Bar ranch so far had taken a beating. Ric then corrected this: the Bar Diamond Bar, as a cattle-ranch, was no more, and hadn't been for the last four years.

After his father's death Ric had tried running the ranch by putting all his faith in his father's old Texas foreman, Shorty Sloan, but Shorty had been killed by a horse going over backwards on him the summer Ric had been home after his first year in Montana U's law school.

Ric had then known it was impossible to run the big ranch and attend college at the same time. He'd laid off fall semester and staged one of Montana's biggest cowroundups.

For three days Bar Diamond Bar had shipped cattle out of Malta, Saco and Hinsdale, down on the Great Northern's rails. He'd homesteaded the ranch buildings, stationed a caretaker there, and had returned to Missoula and the U for the spring semester.

Bar Diamond Bar wasn't taking a beating. Bar Diamond Bar no longer existed except for the strong stone buildings his father had built years before for his Texas bride.

Now both Frances and Brent Williams slept forever under Montana's virgin sod. And their only get faced a hard bucking horse competiton.

Ric looked at the sky. Clouds scurried across it.

Rain fell steadily. Creeks and rivers ran banksful. The soil held all the water it could hold. From now on all rain would be runoff water.

The arena was a quagmire. Muddy water stood in small, deceptive puddles. None of the bucking-horses was shod. A horse could come out of the chute, begin pitching—hit a muddy puddle, and go sliding down, pinning his rider under him.

Ric shrugged.

All in the game, he thought. . . .

III

THE THREE bronc-riding finalists drew to see who would ride first, then second, and then come out of the chute last. Much to Ric's disgust, he drew first ride.

This wasn't good. No matter how well the first bronc-rider rode—or how hard his bronc bucked—usually the excellence of his ride would be lost on the crowd before the last rider hooked his way out of the chute.

The three then drew slips for their horses. Here again Ric found a bit of disappointment for he drew Red Cloud, a sorrel gelding—a bronc not known for his hard bucking.

Greg Mattson drew Mad House, a big bay. Mad House was a tough bucker. Ric had come out on Mad House last year to win first money over Greg and Smokey Smith, a Half Circle V rough-rider.

Hannigan drew the choice horse, the best bucker. The bronc was a big buckskin named Yellow Hell.

Hannigan spoke to Ric. "Yellow Hell? A tough bronc?"

"The best of the three," Ric said. "I'll gladly trade you."

"No trades, cowboys," Malcolm Stewart said. "You ride what you drew, and no other."

Hannigan merely shrugged.

Martha Stewart spoke to Ric. "I'll pick you up, Ric. Which side you want me to ride—right or left?"

"My right," Ric said and added, "Thanks."

Martha smiled her nice smile. "Think nothing of it, cowboy. I like money. You've got a few thousands stashed away, I understand."

She was joking. Or was she?

She referred, of course, to the big sum he'd made by selling out Bar Diamond Bar's ten thousand head of cattle. Ric guessed it was a race between him and Greg Mattson as to who was the richest man on this grass.

Melissa Wentworth sat her horse a few feet away. Naturally she'd heard Martha's joking. She was going to ride pick-up for both Hannigan and Greg Mattson. Ric glanced at her. She was looking at the grandstand's color.

When you rode pick-up you put your horse close to the bronc-rider's bronc and he went from his saddle to yours. These rodeos rules put no time limit on how long a bronc-rider had to stay in saddle.

These rules said you either rode your bronc till he stopped bucking or you were piled.

"Hard earned money," Ric said, grinning.

Ten minutes later he lowered himself down into the saddle on Red Cloud, the big gelding bunching muscles under him. Cautiously, his boots found the oxbow stirrups. Carefully he shifted weight, testing the solidness of the cinch.

The Hamley saddle was screwed down securely. He'd seen to the tightening of the latigo from the ground outside before climbing the chute. The flanking strap was in place.

All three rode the same saddle. Thus none of the three could gain an advantage through using a different hull. This was a flat-plate rig with free and easy stirrup movement.

That meant you could use your spurs high, then rake tough behind—as the rodeo rules demanded.

Ric glanced up. Greg Mattson and Kid Hannigan sat on the corral's top rail some thirty feet away. Both watched him go into the saddle. Ric wondered if this were not the first time he'd seen Kid Hannigan without his gun and gun-belt. You can't keep a gun in holster on a bucking bronc unless you had a tiedown string across its hammer. Otherwise out of leather it would fly.

He saw the gunbelts and guns of Greg Mattson and Kid Hannigan hung over a corral post at Hannigan's right. An amusing thought hit him. Hannigan wasn't far from his weapon.

"Here's your hackamore rope, Williams!" The chute tender snapped his words. "Time you kicked this reprobate outa here!"

Ric twisted the hackamore rope around his right hand, making sure his grip was at least six inches above his saddle's horn.

For if either of your hands touched the horn or the saddle-fork during your ride you were automatically disqualified.

Ric tossed his hat to an onlooker.

"Hold it for me, Sig."

"Sure thing, Ric."

Ric smiled sourly. Butterflies flittered in his belly. His heart beat rather wildly. But the butterflies and the hard beating always were with him when his bronc left the chute.

He lifted both spurs high, saddle-leather

creaking. He felt the big horse's muscles bunch. The horse knew what was ahead.

"Turn him loose," Ric said.

The gate opened. Red Cloud and Ric Nelson met in combat but inside of three lunging jumps out of his bronc Ric knew he was astraddle anything but a winner in this big sorrel.

Red Cloud did his best, but his best wasn't good enough. Ric did his best, but he got little out of his bronc.

Red Cloud bucked toward the grandstand. Ric rode him with disdainful ease. The horse began to run.

Martha rode in close. Ric put his weight on his right stirrup. He put his arms around her slenderness.

He kicked out of his stirrups. Red Cloud ran on with an empty saddle, stirrups flapping. Ric slid to the ground. "No money in that bronc," he said.

"Points," Martha said. "You got quite a few for the other two days. They add up, you know."

"But not high enough, schoolteacher."

Standing there in the rain, Ric Williams bowed to the grandstand. He gauged the applause. Not too much. The grandstand knew a good bronc. The people there were turning thumbs-down on Red Cloud.

He spoke to Malcolm Stewart. "Could I get another bronc?"

Stewart's horse pawed mud. "No other horse, Ric. New rodeo rules this year."

Ric said, cynically, "We live by rules, eh?"

Stewart shrugged. "You should know. You're a law school graduate." He reined his horse around and rode to the bucking chutes where Greg Mattson was testing the cinch on the bucking rig.

For a cowboy had ridden in and snagged Red Cloud by the hackamore rope. Another cowboy had pushed close and unsaddled the bronc and had ridden back with the saddle.

When Ric came up Greg Mattson said, "Damned if that poor buckin' horse didn't almost pile you once or twice, Williams."

Kid Hannigan heard. He still sat on the corral's top rail with a yellow slicker over his shoulders. Kid Hannigan smiled.

Ric said, "You looking for trouble, Mattson?"

"Always," Greg Mattson said, "Always, Williams."

For a long second, violence again hung between Ric Williams and Greg Mattson.

Anger and disappointment was in Ric because of his poor roping and his having drawn a poor bucking-horse. He needed something or somebody to vent this on and Greg Mattson's big jaw was as good a target as any—but then Malcolm Stewart roweled his horse between them.

"This is no prize-fighting ring," the schoolteacher said sharply. "Afterwards you two fools can kill each other, if you want—but right now, Mattson, you got a horse to kick out of that chute, and a few thousand people that have come many miles to see you do it!"

"You don't say, schoolmaster." Greg Mattson's voice dripped sarcasm. Mattson climbed the chute. He looked down at Melissa Wentworth who sat her horse ten feet away. "You pickin' me up, Melissa?"

"If you want me to, Greg."

"Right side, " Greg Mattson said.

He went roughly into leather. His boots found stirrups. He took the hackamore rope from the chute-attendant. He took wraps around his right hand, held his left hand high, raised his spurs and said, "Cut this wolf loose, gentlemen," and Mad House left the chute on a driving, piston-like run, a tough bucking horse.

And Greg Mattson rode him like the bronc-rider he was. One hand high, the other allowing a loose hackamore rope, a Texas trail-drive yell breaking from his leathery throat.

And the grandstand roared.

Mad House swallowed his head. He sunfished, bucked sideways, squealing all the time in rage, ears back, grass-green teeth showing.

Mattson scratched high ahead, then raked his spurs high behind, the big bronc kicking at the flanking strap. Ric Williams watched in admiration. Here was a good bucking horse straddled by a born bronc-rider. Between the two, they made a point-gathering combination.

But all things must end and eventually Mad House ran out of steam. He bucked in front of the grandstand and then stopped, completely beaten. Melissa Wentworth's horse shot in, but Melissa was not needed.

Greg Mattson swung a leg over the saddlehorn and landed on both feet, bowing to the roaring crowd, a wide grin on his sun-tanned handsome face.

He bowed three times, then turned and bowlegged his way back to the bucking chutes, boots grinding mud. He looked at Ric and said, "That'll win first money for me, lawyer."

"Don't count your chickens before they're hatched," Ric said.

Greg Mattson laughed.

The crowd was silent. An air of expectancy held the rainy day. The last bronc-ride was coming up.

Kid Hannigan would come out of Chute Two on Yellow Hell. This ride for the first money was narrowing down.

Ric had won first money the first day on Lost Lady. Greg Mattson had won first the second day bucking-out Loco Gentleman. The second day Ric had won third. The first day Greg Mattson had placed third.

Thus Kid Hannigan had won second two consecutive days. He'd openly grumbled he could easily have won first dough each day had he had a good bucking horse.

Now Hannigan had drawn the range's top bucking-horse. And Black Butte awaited anxiously to see what Hannigan and this bronc would do.

Kid Hannigan slid off the corral-rail to land on his heels in the mud, Garcia spurs jangling.

He tugged at his short beard, grinning.

"Time this boy put his head under the guillotine," he said jokingly.

The three judges—Kitty O'Neill, Sheriff Ratchford and Malcolm Stewart sat their saddles, watching Kid Hannigan. Hannigan went to unbuckle his gunbelt, then remembered he didn't wear it.

"Got so used to it," he told the world, "I feel undressed without it."

Kitty O'Neill said, "Someday this country will get civilized. Then men won't go aroun' with guns tied to their hips to kill each other."

Hannigan said solemnly, "Let's hope thet day comes soon, Miss O'Neill." He handed his hat to the sheriff.

"If'n this bronc kills me," Hannigan said, "thet Stetson is yours, sheriff."

Sheriff Ike Ratchford grinned. "Too small for my big head."

"Then see it lands on a head it fits," Hannigan said grinningly.

"You'll come back," the sheriff said.

The gunman hitched up the belt of the Cheyenne leather chaps. He took his cigarette down, went to throw it away, then apparently thought otherwise, and put the cigarette back between his wind-cracked lips.

He swaggered over to the bucking corral

where wranglers were forcing the big buckskin Yellow Hell into a chute. Once they had the horse pinned in, a man dropped a bar behind the horse's rump, imprisoning him.

Yellow Hell didn't kick or fight back. He'd been through this before. He knew full well what lay ahead. Wisely, he saved his energy. His job was out there in the muddy arena.

Kitty O'Neill and Sheriff Ike rode back to their station. Each judged from a different side of the bucking horse and rider. Malcolm Stewart said, "Time's running by, Kid. They're waiting."

"So is Death."

Tenders were lowering the saddle down on Yellow Hell's broad back. Hannigan caught the cinch as it came swinging in and threaded the latigo strap through the big ring, pulled it tight, and made his tie.

"Don't you want the cinch tighter?" a wrangler asked.

Hannigan shook his head. "He needs to breathe good. Then he can fight harder. You tend to the flankin' strap, pal."

Hannigan climbed the chute. He lowered his chunky frame in the saddle. He fitted his boots into stirrups. He pulled his boots free. "Stirrups need to be shorter," he said.

Stewart reminded, "They're waiting, Kid."

Hannigan had no reply. Handlers hurriedly unlaced stirrup leathers, adjusted them, re-laced them. The gunman tested the length of the stirrup leathers. "That's just right," he said.

Somebody handed him the hackamore rope. For the first time Yellow Hell moved. He put his head downslightly. Hannigan tested the length of the hackamore rope.

"Jus' right."

Stewart said, "Kid, I hate to say it, but—"

"Then don't say it," Hannigan said.

Hannigan lifted both boots high, spurs ready to come down hard on the buckskin's sweaty and rainwet neck.

Hannigan spoke to the buckskin. "You do your best, ol' boy, an' I'll do mine. We need day money and rodeo money. Gotta feed the kitty in Kitty's house." Then, "Turn him loose, men."

The chute gate slid open.

Ric watched in wonder. He was a bronckicker. He'd been reared on a horse. So had been Greg Mattson. Greg was an a-number-one man in the saddle. But never had Ric Williams seen a man ride like the gunman, Kid Hannigan, that rainy, miserable day in May 1899.

Hannigan came out in savage fury. Yellow Hell matched his rider's coldness, inch by inch. Man and horse fought and no quarter was asked or given.

Not a trace of daylight showed between the gunman and the seat of his Hamley saddle. His spurs worked in automatic precision. He rode high on the buckskin's shoulders the necessary five jumps. Then he raked both high in front and high behind.

Ric full well knew that when a man scratched high behind he automatically loosened himself somewhat in his saddle. He was solid in leather on the shoulder hooking, for he had the saddle-fork in front of him, but when he scratched high behind, the saddle's cantle offered little—if any—support.

A rebel yell broke from Kid Hannigan's lips. It was blood curdling, the cattle-trail scream of the Civil War, of the cattle-trails—a sound that had sent terror through the hearts of white and redskin alike.

It had sent terror rippling across the bloodstained grass of Gettysburg. It had been the wild yell of John Welsey Hardin when that Texas gun had made Wild Bill Hickok eat crow and run out of town that Kansas night.

Now it rang across the watching, silent crowd. It washed back from High Black Butte—the rocky northern pinnacle that had given this pioneer town its name.

Kid Hannigan rode with his left hand held high. Never for a second did his hackamore-hand dip even close to the saddle-fork. He and Yellow Hell fought in the middle of the area, the horse's bare-hoofs slapping mud and water.

Once Yellow Hell slipped. Ric saw the horse start down, then catch his balance, and break into wilder bucking. Without thinking, he rode his horse close, intending to pick Hannigan from his saddle when the bronc stopped bucking.

And then, Yellow Hell stopped. He stood, head down, defeated. The crowd went crazy. Never before had Black Butte seen such a bucking horse or such a bronc-rider.

For one long moment, horse and rider were cast in damp broze, outlined motionless against the Montana rain. And, at this moment, Ric Williams rode in, said, "Kid, you did it, you Texas son!"

Hannigan looked at him with small eyes. "Texas, did you say?"

Ric was caught aback. He realized now it had not been his job to pick Hannigan from this buckskin. His admiration for Hannigan as a bronc-rider had overswayed his judgment.

Ric said shortly, "Texas or hell? What the hell difference does it make?"

Hannigan threw back his head. He laughed ironically. He said levelly and clearly, "You can go to hell, Williams!"

Then Hannigan swung his right leg over the saddle-fork to land lightly on his boots in the mud.

He looked momentarily at the howling crowd. Greg Mattson rode in. Hannigan said, "Bunch of damn' idiots." He then spoke to both Ric and Mattson. "That should get me top money for all three days."

He turned and walked through the mud toward the bucking chutes. Once there the first thing he did was buckle on his guns.

Ric Williams scowled.

Hannigan had left the chute with a Bull Durham cigarette between his wind-cracked lips. He'd ridden to a standstill a killer bronc.

And he still smoked the same cigarette. . . .

IV

RIC WILLIAMS split his rodeo-winnings two ways: half to the school, half to the church. Later he heard Greg Mattson had done the same. This did not surprise him.

He and Greg had won money in the annual rodeo since kids on ponies running the barrel-races. Each time their winnings had gone half to the school and half to the town's only church.

Kid Hannigan said he'd deposited his winnings with Kitty O'Neill and was drinking the sum up. Ric had his doubts about this. Hannigan drank, of course—what man didn't?—but he was never seen drunk.

Kid Hannigan was a man of mystery. Despite his bronc-riding, Black Butte did not accept him. Ric figured this normal. These people were clannish and a man had to live within their ranks for twenty years or so to come anywhere close to acceptance.

Or else be born in this area.

Ric Williams figured that soon this clique

would be broken—and forever. The West was becoming civilized. Each day hundreds of European peasants landed in Atlantic ports, lured to the United States by the promises of free land for the asking and personal freedom—especially from terrible, never-ending wars.

Some of these peasants were going into Eastern sweatshops there to work for peanuts a day of twelve hours or more. Some were going directly west to the area of free land for a small U.S. filing fee. Some who had been in this free land for a number of months were quitting the sweatshops and heading west also.

The West was becoming settled. Barbwire and windmills—the two signs of homesteaders—were moving in, encroaching further day by day upon the grass of the cowman and sheepman.

The influx of settlers had begun down in Texas and was working itself north to this section of Montana—only forty miles or so south of the Canuck Line.

These settlers had driven big cattlemen out of Texas and southern Colorado. Barbwire and windmills had forced thousands upon thousands of bony—almost worthless—longhorns north.

Some big cowmen had not given up gracefully. They'd turned gunmen themselves or hired gunmen—and met the homesteaders in gunsmoky battle. Always the homesteaders won.

For one thing, there were too many of the homesteaders. One got killed off and a dozen more took his place. Also, the cattlemen did not own the land they claimed as grazing-land.

This land belonged to Uncle Sam. Cattlemen had moved in free after the rifles had eliminated the millions of buffalos and forced the redman on reservations. What redskins that hadn't wanted to be penned in and robbed of their liberties were ruthlessly slaughtered, following their meal-ticket, the buffalo, into oblivion.

And most of the owners of the big Western cattlespreads had never seen their ranches or the livestock those ranches sported for the owners were in many cases Englishmen and Scotchmen.

Most didn't even know where their big ranches were located. They responded only when the big checks came in each fall for cattle-sales.

Now all this was changing. Down south in Wyoming big cowmen had shipped in a trainload of guns that had gone down before the farmers and social pressure in what is today known as the Johnson County War.

On getting out of high school, Ric Williams had seen this coming. He'd pointed this out to his father who had said no settler would ever set boot on this Black Butte range.

Grizzled old Brent Williams had shaken his head. "Never happen here, son. We're too far away from the railroad. Great Northern is over forty miles south. Nearest shippin' point out is Malta."

"Farmers are settling all along the Milk River along the rails," young Ric had pointed out.

His mother had died of smallpox three years before. Since then old Brent hadn't been quite normal—or so his son had thought. It was tough being the only kid in a family.

It was still tougher when you came late to your father and mother and after they'd even given up the hope of ever having a child.

"Too far away to haul wheat an' supplies in an' out, son."

"Railroads build branch lines."

"Only to where there's freight to be

shipped in and out and the only freight comin' into Black Butte is the bit for the store-and cattle walk out on foot to the cars in Malta."

Schoolteacher Malcolm Stewart had talked Ric into going to Missoula far west in the Rockies and the state university. Ric raised no objections. He didn't like cattle and the cow-business. Leave that for that sap Greg Mattson.

Now he had a law degree, had passed the state bar exams, the U.S. Land Agent —and still no friend to Gregory Watson Mattson, who still nursed cattle along.

And who apparently had been unaware of the menace of barbwire and windmills —until Ric had moved in his three original farmers. George Hess. Jake Mullins. And Ward Griffin.

And now, Jim Young, another farmer on Sage Creek meadows. . . .

"Damn it, sheriff, can't Greg see how things are? How they're going to be?" Ric and Sheriff Ratchford sat in Ric's office.

The stocky lawman spat tobacco-juice out the office's open window. "Greg's no stupid ass, Ric. He's got plenty upstairs."

"I know that. He got better grades than

I did in grammar school, by far. Mr. Stewart will attest to that.

Sheriff Ratchford bit off a fresh chew. "I've talked to him about this thing called *free range* which never was free except it was considered so in the average cowman's brain."

"You have? What did he say?"

"He said he'd buy me another drink."

Ric's face fell. Greg Mattson had clever ways of evading questions. Most of the time he answered a question by asking another question in true politician fashion.

"There's room for cattle and there always will be," Ric said.

Sheriff Ratchford's faded eyes studied him. "You're dealin' in contradictions, son."

Ric shook his head. "No, I'm not. The world cannot exist without livestock. Bovines are livestock. But the longhorn—" He shook his head.

The lawman nodded. "I understan'. Longhorns eat more forage than two Herefords and produce about one-quarter the meat, if that much. You can fatten two good blooded Herefords where you can keep one longhorn skinny and almost worthless for the market."

"And cattle can graze on land that isn't

fit for farming or is too rough to farm," Ric said.

"Greg's trailin' in some full-blooded polled shorthorn bulls."

Ric's brows rose.

"From Canady," the sheriff said.

"He tell you that?"

"That he did. Should be in sometime next week. Aroun' twenty odd head, he said."

"Why from the Canucks?"

"Closest place they is such. He had to dicker quite a bit with the Canuck officials, I understand. They don't want what little hot-blooded stock they got leavin' their country."

Ric did a little arithmetic in months. A cow needed nine months from breeding to calfing. Usually a cow in this cold country threw her calf in April or May—or maybe even in late March, but in late March was risky for a late blizzard might hit and freeze the little newcomer to death.

Most cowmen turned their bulls out with their cows in June. Thus cows threw calves in early spring. By fall the youngsters were big enough to shift through the winter without their mother's milk and with a handful of hay now and then.

The terrible winter of 1886-87 had taught both Brent Williams and Greg's father that the cattle-business could not be carried on this far north without an outfit cutting hay in the summer to tide cattle through the long and terribly cold Montana winters.

That winter had completely wiped out Teddy Roosevelt on his little Missouri ranch just outside of Montana's eastern border. The politician from New York State had immediately given up the cattle-business as a bad job and retired to being no more than a politician.

Some northern cattlemen after that terrible winter had even sold off what few cattle that had survived and stocked their range lands with sheep on the premise that woolies could stand hard winters better than longhorns.

This had proven a grievous error. This logic had been based on two points: the thick woolen coat of the sheep and the fact that sheep could eat grass closer to the roots than cattle.

Their thick wool protected sheep, yes—but sheep could graze no closer under heavy snow than a cow. Neither a cow or a sheep would paw the snow away to get to what little grass lay under the white blanket. A horse would paw down to earth and find

53

what little grass there was. Neither a sheep or cow will do this.

They will graze only what grass—if any—that rears its tops through the snow. And naturally when snow is a few feet deep no grass raises up to feed a cow or a sheep.

Stockmen soon learned that sheep would drift with a blizzard until they piled up against a cutbank or hill and eventually were completely covered by snow. Sheep for some reason froze to death faster than a cow.

Also woolies were fair game for wolves, coyotes, bobcats and mountain lions, not to mention roving grizzly bears. Cattle fought off predators. Sheep stood and offered no resistance when being killed by wild animals.

Sheep had one advantage over cattle, though. A ewe created two incomes a year for its owner while a cow created only one. The cow produced a calf, and there its value ceased—but a sheep had wool for sale and in the fall the lamb—if a wether—went to market.

And the price of mutton—and wool—was very unstable. Australia and other nations began to produce wool and mutton, sending the market price down—and some former cattlemen got rid of their woolies and went back to cattle.

"I don't want any trouble with Greg and his Half Circle V riders," Ric told the sheriff. "I go on official record here and now on that point, Mr. Ratchford."

"You don't need to have such, Ric."

"How come you say that?"

"Well, let's say Greg makes a move. It won't be against you personally. Unless I'm cockeyed it'll be against the farmers."

"I agree," Ric said, "but I'm responsible for those hoemen, as Greg calls them. I got them in here. I settled them on homesteads. I surveyed and marked off the limit of those homesteads. Any blow against the farmers is automatically a blow against me."

"I understand. . . . I'll talk to Greg."

Ric shook his head. "Won't do a bit of good. He and I have already discussed this problem."

The sheriff's brows rose. "Oh. . . . Where, might I ask—and when?"

"In Kitty's saloon. He was in a poker game with Melissa Wentworth, her table. A couple of others in it, too. I bought a couple of bucks of chips opposite Greg."

Sheriff Ratchford listened.

"Greg and I had some conversation—not much—across the table. I asked him to visit

55

me in my office. He just grunted something, no more. I told him I'd gladly ride the ten miles to Half Circle V to talk to him. He told me not to waste my horse. Things started to freeze up. Vern Wood was in the game. He pulled out. I got out, too—or I'd have broken up Melissa Wentworth's table, and I didn't want to do that."

"Greg claims Half Circle V's been losin' cattle."

Ric Williams studied the lawman's rugged face. "I've heard that rumor, too—not direct from Greg, but from others. Do you think it's true, sheriff?"

"Greg's an honest man. He's like his father, Scott Mattson. If Greg says his spread's been losin' stock, I'll say it's been losin' cattle."

Ric mulled this over. Greg Mattson had just finished his spring calf-branding roundup.

Greg evidently had also run a count on his cattle—cows, steers, bulls and calves—during the gather. Spring had come late this year. Greg and his cowboys had had to ride some cold circles.

"What did he find out, sheriff?"

Sheriff Ratchford got slowly afoot. "Bones gettin' ol' an' stiff." He spoke to the world in general. "I'm gettin' like an ol' hoss that's been run fast down too many slants—stiff in the muscles." He looked out one of the windows at Black Butte. "Town never changes. Same buildin's, jus' older."

"It'll soon change. Farmers will change it."

"You asked me a question?" Ric repeated.

"Greg took a tally last fall when Half Circle V did its beef-gather. He compared that count to the one this spring. About six hundred head short, he tol' me."

Ric whistled softly. "Hard winter, though—and lots of winter-kill."

Sheriff Ratchford shook his grizzled head. "Yes, lots of stock went under, 'specially after that late March blizzard. But Greg told his cowboys while on circle to tally all the dead carcasses they ran acrost, which they did."

"What did this tally show?"

"Far from six hundred."

Ric scowled. He played with a pencil. "All right, let's do a little surmising, sheriff."

"Go ahead."

"Wouldn't be much of a chore to get

hold of cattle during a winter as rough as the last one."

"Get a hayrack ahead full of hay—dole off a forkful now an' then an' every cow in the Black Butte area would foller you to where you wanted her to go."

Ric got to his boots. He went to the sink and turned on the faucet and got a tincup full of clear water. Black Butte town was one of the few small towns in this section that had running water in its houses.

His father and Scott Mattson had seen to that. On the south base of Black Butte hill was a spring that never went dry. Directly below the spring the two pioneers had built a rock and concrete reservoir.

They'd then piped from the spring into the reservoir and then had run pipes downhill to the town they'd laid out and built.

Ric drank of the cold water, hung his cup on the hook, and looked out the window. The rain was slacking off. He was glad of that. The earth held all the water it could. The remainder just ran into creeks and the river and made a flood threat.

Sheriff Ratchford was correct. Black Butte hadn't changed since being built. The only thing that had occurred was that the town's buildings had grown older and many now needed paint.

Ric turned. "All right, let's say—for the record—that Greg Mattson's been losing cattle. Where would they go?"

"Feed the Indians on reservations, mebbe so?"

Ric considered that. Within a radius of fifty miles there were three or four Indian reservations. Two were big ones with quite a few inhabitants—the Assiniboine and the Gros Ventres.

Army sutlers bought beef for these many hungry mouths. And an army sutler didn't care what type of beef the redman ate as long as he—the sutler—bought that meat cheap and sold it dear to unsuspecting Uncle Sam.

Rumor was that the sutler cut in the army officials on his profit. And the Indian got the boniest, oldest beef that could be bought—a far cry from the juicy thick buffalo steaks of just a few years ago.

"The army books are open to the public," Ric said. "All a man had to do was ask and he'd see."

The lawman laughed shortly. "That's what the law says, yes—but when you look at a ledger, how do you know it tells the truth?"

"You mean the generals—and the sutlers—sometimes keep two sets of books?"

"They sure do. An' they give you the doctored one—the one they submit each year to Uncle Sam."

"They have to skin cows before eating them," Ric pointed out. "A man might be able to get hold of a hide and see its brand."

"I doubt that. Those boys are smart. I gotta hunch they'd get rid of them hides right off the bat. Either bury them deep, burn them up with acid—or get them outa the country in a hell of a hurry."

"Or change brands? Half Circle V could be easy turned into a Circle Diamond. Complete the half circle, put a V over the first V—and presto, Circle Diamond, sheriff."

The sheriff nodded.

"Where else could stolen cattle go?" Ric asked.

"Across the line. Canady."

Ric thumbed his bottom lip. "That's right. Miles and miles of unmarked territory and not a U.S. man or Mountie in sight. . . . Rebrand like I said and drive north. As simple as that."

"Brands are registered in Canady," the sheriff pointed out.

"Some are," Ric said, "and some aren't, maybe?"

"That could easily be."

Ric sat down, nerves restless. This was a new land. It had a long, long way to go to become a legal, law-abiding country. Although the people—some of them, that was—tried to bring in law and order, it was an uphill fight. It could go either way.

It all depended on the people.

Newcomers could—and would—tip the balance either way. If evil-minded newcomers arrived, evil would remain dominant. If good people homesteaded and settled, peace and order would win out.

Most of the homesteaders were good, church-going people who wanted to eke out a living from the land and live with their families in peace. Ric's mind went to his three cowpuncher-farmers.

Evidently the sheriff's mind had taken the same turn for Sheriff Ratchford said, "Naturally, Greg's suspicious of those three farmers you settled on Hell Crick last fall."

"Hess, Mullins and Griffin?"

"That's the three. What'd you know about them?"

Ric considered this momentarily. "Nothing besides that they paid their filing fees and I found the section-line markers."

"This past winter? You kept an eye on 'em?"

"Not in the way you refer to, sheriff. Should I have?"

"I don't know. I'm a lawman. I've been a law-officer since a young man. And to an officer of the law each person is guilty until proven innocent, the reverse of normal procedure."

"A man never knows," Ric said.

Sheriff Ratchford stopped just inside the open door. "I've talked to a couple of eye-witnesses to that Young-Hannigan trouble. A couple wouldn't commit themselves but the others say like Hannigan—that this Young button deliberately staggered against Hannigan."

"He was drunk," Ric pointed out.

The sheriff shook his head slowly. "But not that drunk—in my estimation, anyway."

"He's no fool. At least, he doesn't seem a fool to me. So why would he be anxious to commit suicide?"

Sheriff Ratchford shrugged. "Let's leave that rest for a while, Ric. We're in an area of homestead boundaries and the Homestead Law. God bless Honest Abe for making that federal law. How about this town? Who owns the land the town sits on?"

"The town does. It's incorporated and the land patented. My father and Greg's dad saw to that immediately. Nobody from outside can touch it. Each householder owns the lot his property is on."

"But your father and Scott Mattson are dead."

"That makes no difference. The patent reads that with their deaths the property remains intact in the name of each and every householder—original householders, that is."

"What if newcomers come in and want to build?"

"They buy from the town council. You're a member of that. The money goes into the Town Improvement Fund."

"You still own Bar Diamond Bar buildings. Did your father ever homestead the land the buildings sit on?"

"He sure did. Dad missed nothing. He homesteaded that one-hundred and sixty the first year he was in those buildings."

"How about Scott Mattson? Did he homestead the land where Half Circle V has its buildings?"

"I don't think so. I could check by getting word to the U.S. Land Office in Great Falls. Seems to me I remember Dad saying he'd tried to get Scott Mattson to homestead and Mattson said this land would never be homesteaded—that it was worthless as farmland and no farmers would ever come in."

"That sounds like ol' Scott. Bullheaded as a longhorn bull. Then if it isn't homesteaded a man could stake out a claim where Greg's buildin's are—and claim the land and buildin's, an' all?"

"That's right."

"Somebody should ask Greg to make sure he owns the land where his buildin's are. Those buildin's are worth money."

"Anybody try to homestead that land and it would mean bullets," Ric said.

"Not while I'm the law. An' if all is legal. Why don't you question Greg about this?"

Ric laughed shortly. "You want a gunfight in your bailiwick? Old Doc Myers once lectured on the breakdown of social relations. He said that when means of communication were gone, there was nothing left but violence."

"Who's Doc Myers?"

"The best prof at the U."

V

THE RAIN stopped. The sun came out. Grass sprang up. What had been only bare earth suddenly became green and verdant.

Creeks and rivers went down to normal. Meadowlarks sang. Wild flowers stuck heads up through thick grass. Crocuses, wild sweet-peas, blue-bells. Meadowlarks built nests in sagebrush.

Soon young sagehens appeared. When they were approached by man or another peril the mother clucked her chickens into hiding and flew away as if a wing were broken in an attempt to lure the danger away from her new family.

Stupid dogs lunged after the mother sagehen, thinking she was wounded and they'd soon catch her. When a proper distance away from her chickens she'd suddenly recover the use of her injured wing.

And away she would sail, leaving the ignorant canine behind to wonder how she'd recuperated so suddenly—but this ruse did not fool an experienced and wise coyote.

The coyote knew she was only playing tricks. He knew she had full use of both wings and was only pulling danger away from her young. He put his nose to the ground and went to work.

Ric Williams knew that a man could step on a young sagehen chicken without seeing it, the chicken being the color of the earth. Only as the last resort, the moment just before the foot came down that would crush him to death, did the chick run for safety.

But the coyote didn't depend on his sight. He depended on the smelling power of his long, bony nose. And when the chicken did come out of hiding, he came too late—and too slowly.

For the coyote soon had the chicken between his jaws.

A similar fate also was met by many a young prairie chicken. The grouse was smarter. She built her nest in the brush along creeks and rivers. And the coyote didn't like brush. He'd get tangled in the wild rose bushes and thorny buckbrush. So he stayed on the sagebrush and greasewood covered land—and here nested the sagehen and the prairie chicken.

Within a few days the sides of Black Butte turned from brown to green. Even its flinty crest sported a bit of green, Ric Williams noticed. Three days after the rains quit three lumber-wagons—laden with various household goods—pulled laboriously into Black Butte.

"Sodbusters comin', Ma!"

"Three wagonloads of them darn farmers, Pa!"

Ric stared at the wagons, his heart picking up a beat. Plainly the three wagons belonged to three would-be farmers. Each wagon carried a cast-iron cook-stove. Yes, and some old furniture, too. A table, some chairs, a cupboard—things like that.

All of Black Butte came out not to welcome but to stare. People appeared in doorways and on the plank sidewalks. The wagons ground in halfway to the hubs in drying earth and all stopped in front of Ric's land-office and law-office.

The man on the lead wagon said, "You perhaps is Mr. Richard Williams, sir?" He spoke in a soft drawl. The *sir* became *suh* in his bearded mouth.

"That I am," Ric assured.

"My name's Smith Jones. The man on the second wagon there—the one ahin' mine—is John Rogers. An' the tail wagon's the property of Bob Winston, Mr. Williams."

"Pleased to meet you, Mr. Jones."

Ric went from wagon to wagon, shaking hands. Jones was short and solid looking with a beard. He and Kid Hannigan were the two only bearded men in this area.

Ric wondered why he had this errant thought. Then he remembered Kid Hannigan and Greg Mattson riding into town about half an hour ago. They'd ridden past his office, horses fiddle-footing and dancing despite the mud.

Mattson had not looked at Ric, standing in his office's open door, but Kid Hannigan had ironically lifted the hand holding his reins, the usual look of cynicism on his bearded lips.

Ric had lifted his hand slightly in return. The two had gone into the post office—which was in the Merc—and then had boot-hammered their way downstreet to Kitty O'Neill's saloon.

John Rogers was a lanky man with a prominent Adam's-apple. Bob Winston was the youngest, Ric figured—a redheaded burly man of around thirty with many freckles.

"We come out to get located on homesteads, Mr. Williams," Winston informed.

John Rogers said, "We shipped our junk into Malta. Mr. Maresh there tol' us to come out to your town."

Clarence Maresh was U.S. area land agent in the county seat down on Great Northern rails. He was a busy man what with many settlers arriving each day to settle on river homesteads along Milk River which ran east and west through Montana in this region.

"He couldn't locate us along the river 'cause all thet land there is took up," Smith Jones informed. "He said you had some good lan' along a crick called Sage Crick you could locate us on."

Martha Stewart left the Merc and stood beside Ric. Ric was glad she'd come to his side. He'd felt rather alone and lost for long moment.

That morning the stage had gone south on its run down from Timber Mountain, across the Canadian Line, in Saskatchewan Province. It had rocked down into Black Butte at five, depositing two salesmen and a drunken cowboy looking for a punching job at its depot, Kitty O'Neill's saloon.

The stage had carried south to Malta a letter Ric had posted the afternoon before addressed to his boss, Mr. Maresh, in Malta. This letter had outlined the trouble extant in Black Butte and had asked the senior land-officer to send no more settlers north to Black Butte until this trouble had been settled, if it ever would be.

The letter would reach Malta this evening. These men had apparently left Malta yesterday morning. Ric figured the trip north had taken them two days because of the rutted road and the distance.

"Oh, lord," he said under his breath.

Martha heard him. "Why say that, Ric?" She spoke so softly nobody heard but Ric.

"Greg Mattson," Ric said.

"Here he comes now," the schoolteacher said. "And he has Kid Hannigan with him."

Ric glanced upstreet toward Kitty's saloon. Onlookers stood on the saloon's long front porch and watched. Greg Mattson and Kid Hannigan were heading toward Ric's office.

"Somethin' wrong, Mr. Williams?" Smith Jones asked.

"We have a little problem," Ric confessed. "Just drop your lines and come into my office, please?"

"Me an' Finn'll watch their teams an' rigs," Sonny Hanson said and added, "for a nickel apiece, of course."

Ric smiled. "Of course, Sonny."

The three farmers entered Ric's office, Smith Jones in the lead, Bob Winston holding down the rear.

"Sit down," Ric invited.

The farmers sat. They were tense and stiff. Ric's sudden change of attitude upon seeing Greg Mattson and Kid Hannigan come from the saloon puzzled them. What was going on here, anyway?

Ric stayed in the doorway, facing the street. Sheriff Ike Ratchford left the barber shop directly across the street and hurried toward Ric's office.

Ric glanced at the Merc. Malcolm Stewart was coming his way. Ric breathed easier now.

He knew full well that neither Stewart nor Ratchford favored his cause more than the cause of Greg Mattson. Ratchford hurried this direction because keeping peace was his elected job.

Stewart came because he loved peace and tranquility. He was a great advocate of compromise, not force.

Ratchford stopped on the edge of the

plank sidewalk. Stewart halted thirty feet upstreet.

Greg Mattson and Kid Hannigan passed Stewart. He looked at them and they looked at him and Mattson said, "You move fast for a man your age, schoolteacher."

Stewart said, "I'm the type of man who ages slowly."

Martha stood beside Ric. Ric looked beyond Greg Mattson and Kid Hannigan. Kitty O'Neill had left her saloon and was walking rapidly in Ric's direction. Ric looked beyond the square-built saloon-keeper.

Melissa Wentworth also came this direction, but not at the rapid pace her boss assumed. Again Ric, despite the distance, saw and admired the blonde loveliness of the card dealer and her thin waist.

Martha Stewart saw Ric's admiring glance. Ric did not see her scowl because his eyes had moved to Greg Mattson and Kid Hannigan.

The pair stopped in front of Ric, and Greg Mattson looked about and said, "Seems as if when me an' the Kid headed this way the whole damn' town came alive an' headed this way too."

Ric had no answer. He looked at bearded Kid Hannigan. The Kid stood a pace behind his boss and three paces to Greg Mattson's left. He had both thumbs hooked idly in front of his wide, cartridge-loaded gunbelt.

Greg Mattson looked at the sheriff. He said "Howdy, Ike," and Ratchford said, "Howdy, Greg. An' you too, Kid Hannigan."

"I thank you, sheriff, " Hannigan said.

Greg looked at Malcolm Stewart, then at Kitty O'Neill, still on her way, and beyond Kitty at Melissa Wentworth, hurrying to catch Kitty. An ironic smile touched his wind-cracked lips.

He turned his gray eyes back to Ric. "Three farmers—newcomers—inside, Ric?"

Ric nodded.

Greg Mattson said shortly, "Cat eat your tongue, Williams? Or are you afraid to open your mouth when among men?"

Greg Mattson's voice was heavy with sarcasm. Once again Ric Williams felt the old anger rise. Had this occurred on the grammar school playground ten years ago he would have immediately tied into this arrogant young rancher.

The thought came that he and Greg Mattson had not tangled in a fistfight since he'd come home from college. Greg might find him a different opponent now, one who definitely could handle his fists much better than before going to college.

Ric had told nobody around here that at the university his junior and senior years he'd been light-heavyweight champ of the conference the university belonged to.

He'd taken a beating getting to the top of his weight class, but he'd finally made it. He laid much of the ability to take pain and fight back to his schoolyard fights with Greg Mattson.

"Cat ate my tongue," he said.

His eyes caught Ratchford's. The sheriff nodded slightly. That told Ric he was on the right track.

Nobody spoke for a long moment. Kid Hannigan stood stolid and silent, eyes darting here, then there, back again. Suddenly, without warning, Greg Mattson laughed softly—but anger lurked behind the laugh's seeming gentleness.

"I only came here for one purpose, Williams. Not to look over these farmers an' warn them, as you folks all expected."

Ric's brows rose, but he asked no questions.

"I understan' you hinted that the land my

ranch buildin's set on ain't homesteaded." Greg Mattson spoke to Ric Williams.

Ric said honestly, "I haven't the slightest idea. My father homesteaded Bar Diamond Bar's homesite right after building but I don't know about your father—he might have homesteaded Half Circle V land, or not. It's none of my business."

"I talked to Greg," Sheriff Ratchford told Ric.

Ric nodded.

Greg Mattson said, "I've searched all the old man's records. I can't find anythin' thet points towards his homesteadin' thet land. I'm purty sure he never homesteaded it."

Ric said, "Sometimes that happens." His innate anger was falling in face of the fact that this cowman—and his hired gun—apparently constituted no danger . . . not at the present, at least.

"I'm goin' to make sure it's under homestead," Greg Mattson told the onlookers. "Therefore I'm homesteadin' it myself, even if the records do come up that my father also used his homestead rights on it."

Nobody spoke.

The big young cowman looked back at Ric Williams. "What do I do first to pertect my right?"

"Come back in about an hour," Ric said. "I'll be through with these newcomers then."

"What's the procedure?" Greg Mattson disregarded Ric's words.

"First you file a notice with me you wish to homestead. I then make sure you're eligible."

"I'm over twenty-one, a citizen, an'—"

"There'll be no reason you can't file," Ric said hurriedly. "An hour, then?"

"On the point," Greg Mattson said. "Come on, Hannigan."

"Okay, boss."

The two headed back toward Kitty's saloon. Greg pulled fresh and clean good air deep into his lungs.

The townspeople drifted away, leaving only Malcolm Stewart, his daughter, and Sheriff Ratchford with Ric.

The day was anything but hot and yet the sheriff mopped his wide forehead with his blue bandanna. "Sweat easy lately," he told the world. "Gettin' ol', I reckon."

He turned and crossed the street to the barbershop. He had a checker game waiting there, Ric knew.

Malcolm Stewart said, "Back to the Merc

with me. Helping them clean out the back storeroom."

Dark feminine eyes looked up at Ric. Martha Stewart said, "I was on my way to Grandma Hay's house. She's down with her bad leg again."

Ric said, "I thank you, Martha."

"For what?"

"Well—" Ric hesitated.

Martha sighed. "I wish someday men would finally get civilized."

"That day," Ric said, "might never come."

She continued down the street. Ric admired her waist. Not quite as small as Melissa's, but indeed a pretty waist.

He grinned and turned and entered his office. His new clients still sat where he'd left them.

"I got a feelin' there's trouble here," bearded Smith Jones said.

Ric explained everything including young Jim Young's run-in the last week with Kid Hannigan. The farmers listened in silence. Ric finished and John Rogers' Adam's apple moved up and down as he said, "Jim's a man who can't handle his booze."

Ric looked at Rogers. "You talk as though you know Jim Young."

Rogers explained. He and Jones and Winston had worked on the Detroit police with Jim Young. "His letters back home is what got us three out here," Rogers finished.

Ric was slightly surprised. Jim Young had told him nothing about writing home and recommending Black Butte range. Young's letters had apparently convinced each of these ex-police that Sage Creek was the right spot for them to take up homesteads.

Ric then explained the predicament Young was in by settling on grass and water claimed by Half Circle V. Freckle-faced Bob Winston then said, "On the way out we seen lots of native grass an' the cricks were runnin' bankful, Mister Williams."

Ric told about the long rainy season. "That doesn't happen often and at the right time," he told them.

Once again John Rogers' Adam's apple went up and down. "Jim tol' us about thet in his letters. He says Sage Crick can be dammed—jus' a small diversion dam—and it could irrigate hundreds of acres of head crops, the land on each side of the crick bein' that flat."

Jim Young was right. With the least rain

Sage Creek Meadows became flooded by the creek which had very, very low banks. The flooding and washing in of new alluvial soil was what made the Meadows so worthy to Half Circle V ranch.

For after each spring or summer flooding, bluejoint grass immediately grew high on the level land. Half Circle V mowers then went into action, mowing the grass for winter feed.

Rakes came along and bunched the hay. Bullrakes then came and picked it up and threaded their tines into the tines of the stacker before backing away, leaving the hay on the stacker bed.

A workhorse then pulled the stacker into the air where it deposited its hay on the growing haystack—and its resultant use as fodder for cattle when snow came and covered the range's brown grass.

"Jim's surveyed that country," Smith Jones said.

Ric's brows rose. "Surveyed?"

"Yeah. Jim's an odd duck. Always readin' an' when he was back in Detroit he always went to night classes at some school to learn somethin'—bookkeepin', surveyin', something about crops. Things like that."

All three were anxious to see Jim Young.

There was nothing more that Ric could do. He warned them of the Half Circle V menace. Each said he was a good shot. Ric didn't doubt that a bit. Detroit had some tough sections, he'd heard.

A Detroit cop had to be tough . . . or be killed.

Each had filed preliminary papers down at Mr. Maresh's office. All the papers lacked was a legal description of the homesteads each wanted.

Ric walked to the big wall map. He showed them the lay of the land. Black Butte town was here on the west side of Black Butte river and on the southeast flank of Black Butte peak.

His pointer pointed here, then there. He felt like a schoolteacher teaching geography. He pointed where Sage Creek entered Black Butte River, a mere quarter mile south of Black Butte town.

His pointer traveled the length of Sage Creek almost due west forty miles up the creek.

"You got other farmers settled?" Smith Jones asked.

"Three others. They came in last fall. They're ex-cowpunchers, I'd say—anyway, they look like ex-cowpunchers. They're north of Sage Creek—" His pointer traveled up the map. "—on Hell Creek."

The new farmers watched. John Rogers said, "Hell Creek comes into Sage jus' a few miles west of Jim Young's homestead, eh?"

"That it does," Ric said.

Bob Winston looked at the area east of Black Butte River, his eyes on Greasewood Creek which ran into Black Butte River and half-mile north of Black Butte town.

"Ain't got no farmers out thet way east?" Winston asked. "Can't see where you've blocked out homestead limits there, Mister Williams."

"No settlers out there yet," Ric informed, "but they'll come. That's sagebrush land and sagebrush land is good land. Land that grows greasewood has too much alkali in it to raise good crops—both white and black alkali."

The farmers got to their boots. They'd drive their loaded wagons out to Jim Young's homestead and spend the night there. "I'll meet you tomorrow morning there," Ric promised.

The new farmers trooped toward the door. Ric looked at his watch. An hour had passed. Greg Mattson should be arriving. He knew from school days that Greg was never late. Greg's parents saw to that.

Ric looked up. Greg Mattson stood in the doorway. He was big, hard-looking, gun-hung, booted, spurred. Behind him stood his gunman, Kid Hannigan. And, as usual, the bearded Hannigan had both thumbs hooked in his gunbelt's front.

The farmers stopped. Greg Mattson and Hannigan blocked the doorway. Smith Jones headed the new farmers. Behind him was John Rogers, then Bob Winston.

Silence fell.

VI

THE FARMERS faced Greg Mattson and Kid Hannigan.

Greg Mattson and the gunman faced the new farmers. The farmers wore no guns. Half Circle V was gun-hung, dangerous.

Smith Jones broke the silence with, "With your pardon, gentlemen, we three would like to leave."

Greg Mattson didn't move an inch.

Smith Jones looked at Ric Williams. "I believe this is the Mr. Mattson you warned us about, Mr. Williams?"

Ric stepped forward. "It is, Mr. Jones." Then, to Greg Mattson, "These men want to leave. I'm sorry I kept them more than an hour. We had a lot to talk over—"

"Let 'em leave, then!" Greg Mattson moved to one side, just inside the door.

The farmers walked out. Kid Hannigan, out on the sidewalk, moved back a pace, eyes on the farmers. He spoke from the corner of his mouth to his boss inside Ric's office. "You need me any more, boss?"

"I don't need you, Kid," Greg Mattson said.

"Then I'll be headin' back to Miss Melissa's poker game," Kid Hannigan said. "Still got a bit of the rodeo winnin's burnin' holes in my pocket."

Kid Hannigan turned and went north and out of sight. Ric watched his farmers momentarily out a window. They were climbing onto the high seats.

He said to Greg Mattson, "Sit down."

"I'm sittin'," Greg Mattson said.

Smith Jones saw Ric in the window. He grinned and lifted his lash and sent it cracking over the heads of his horses. The team hit collars. Ric noticed the lash had not hit a horse. The snapping bullet-like report of the bullwhip had wakened the broncs to quick life, though.

The wagons went out of sight.

Ric spoke to Greg Mattson. "Your father might have homesteaded your ranch buildings. I could check with the U.S. Land Office in Helena."

Mattson shook his head. "I homesteaded it today. Mebbeso the old man didn't file papers? Then if he didn't some worthless farmer could come in, file on the property's site, and own the buildings.

"Your claim might prove false if there's an original homestead."

Greg Mattson's gray eyes looked at Ric Williams. "What the hell you tryin' to pull off, Williams? Another of your old shady deals, mebbeso?"

Ric's temper rose. His cheekbones reddened. He breathed deeply and said, "You come here for trouble, Mattson?"

"I came here to file a homestead. You seem to want to refuse to accept my filin'. But if it's trouble you want here I am, bucko!"

Ric caught his temper. "Okay, you make out filing papers. Here they are. You pay the filing fee, just like everybody else. And tomorrow morning I'll go out and find the township cornerstone and work back from it to your buildings and run out your one hundred and sixty acres of homestead."

"How much is the filin' fee?"

"Twenty bucks."

"Who gets it?"

"Uncle Sam gets half. I get the other half. What're you bellyachin' about? You've got lots of money."

"So have you, Williams."

"And I didn't earn a bit of it. I inherited it all. My father's sweat and blood, not mine. And the same goes for you, Mattson."

"Don't you like it?"

"I'd feel a hell of a lot better if I'd made it myself instead of having it given to me."

For one moment Greg Mattson's handsome face showed something—but only for a brief clocktick. "You got a point there, Williams, much as I hate to admit it."

Ric sighed. "Fill out that form and if you have any questions ask me, Mattson."

"This question, here—the one askin' for boundaries."

"We don't know what they are yet. I'll know when I make my survey in the morning. I'll fill that in, then."

"Okay."

Greg Mattson wet the pencil's lead. Ric walked to the window and looked out on Black Butte. The sheriff had been right. The town looked shabby. It needed repairs and some new paint.

For the hundredth time he wondered if he'd done right by coming back to Black Butte after getting his law degree. He could have stayed in Missoula or gone to Butte or Great Falls and set up a law office. He'd graduated high in the small class and had

had various offers of good jobs in all three of these big Montana towns.

The junior U.S. Senator had even asked him to go to Washington, D.C. as his secretary, hinting that soon his secretary would be reading law for a supreme court judge.

Yet Ric had turned down all these offers and returned to the hate and strife of his old home town. He wondered why. His two relatives here—mother and father—slept in silent graves. He ran no more cattle. Weekends he rattled around the big Bar Diamond Bar ranch-house.

Weekdays a caretaker watched over the big buildings. Ric then realized the only time he felt really at peace with himself and the world was when he was at the ranch.

Lately a number of thoughts had pestered him, thoughts he'd got from reading pamphlets on farming sent out by Uncle Sam's Department of Agriculture—most of them concerned with irrigation of the West's arid lands.

Uncle Sam's engineers advocated check dams. These were small dams with spillways you built at the mouths of ravines and coulees. When rains came the dams impounded the precious water.

If there was too much rain, it ran harmlessly over the concrete spillway—thus keeping the dam from being washed out.

Each dam had a headgate. A ditch could be built to the headgate and the stored water could be directed downhill onto fields.

Greg Mattson asked, "This question here, shyster?"

The word *shyster* rankled Ric Williams. A shyster was a crooked lawyer. Ric knew Mattson deliberately had sandpapered him. For one wild moment he also fell for the bait.

Then common sense came and established control. He overlooked the insulting word.

He walked over and looked at the question. It was simply a *yes* or *no* deal, very simple. Mattson had deliberately sought to pull him into a trap. Had he done so, Ric's office would have now been in a process of destruction.

Ric gave the answer. He returned to the window, mind on check-dams. Uncle Sam's boys knew their stuff. The state's U.S. Land Office would send out engineers to do the surveying and scouting . . . and for free, he knew.

He remembered the low hills south of his ranch. They drained quite an area. Their coulees afforded good areas in which to build dams. The land below sloped gradually north.

With check-dams, and a little rain, he had a hunch he could turn the acres south of the ranchhouse—and those surrounding it on the west, north and east—into a wonderful irrigated farm.

He had discovered these government pamphlets during his senior year in college. He'd learned all the information regarding such as he could from profs in civil engineering and forestry, for the forest service, he had learned, made much use of small check-dams.

Through ranch records he'd learned that his mother, Augusta Williams, had years ago filed on a homestead south of her husband's land. This gave her son control of the southern hills and their potential water.

Ric had then filed for his own homestead to abut his father's land on the north. This gave him three-quarters of a mile of land half a mile wide from the foothills north.

He'd also learned he could file claim for four hundred and eighty more acres in his own name. This he'd promptly done. These papers were now being processed in the state's U.S. Land Office.

When all was done and paid for he'd own a piece of land a mile wide and a mile and half long, running north and south with the ranch-house in its approximate middle.

But time was dragging. To prove-up on a homestead certain improvements must be made for Uncle Sam to witness, and a fence was one of these. He decided that in the morning he'd look for a few workers who would go out and dig post holes and cut diamond-willow posts along the river to build a three wire fence around the entire acreage.

He'd get the Merc to order the necessary barbwire from Malta. With Greg Mattson's spring roundup finished there were bound to be men looking for work in town for between roundups and during winters big ranches had little use for many men—thus cowpunchers without a job.

Ric came back from prospective fields of sweet-blooming alfalfa when Greg Mattson pushed back his chair and said, "That should be it."

Ric studied the application. He had Mattson make a few changes here and there. "I'll be out in the morning at eight sharp."

"How about these new farmers? Where they settlin'?"

"On Sage Creek. Around Jim Young.

They're ex-cops from Detroit, all friends of Young."

"Young got 'em out here, eh?"

"I don't ask my clients as to their personal affairs," Ric said. "I only ask enough questions—and demand enough proof—of their eligibility to homestead, nothing more."

"An' collect filin' fees," Greg Mattson said.

"That's right. And you owe me twenty bucks."

Greg Mattson dug out his wallet. He threw a double-eagle on Ric's desk. "In the mornin'," he said.

"In the morning," Ric assured.

Mattson strode out, spurs jingling. Ric studied the application again. He noticed Greg Mattson was just a few days older than he. He thought of Sage Creek Meadows.

Sage Creek Meadows was actually on range once claimed by Bar Diamond Bar for Scott Mattson and Brent Williams had fixed an unmarked border between their two ranches directly after turning the Texas longhorns in on this Montana grass.

This boundary line cut straight east and west through the middle of Black Butte. Thus the town of Black Butte actually had been inside of land claimed by the Williams' iron.

Thus also Sage Creek Meadows would be on land claimed through squatter's right by Brent and Augusta Williams. So also would be Hell Creek three miles north of its junction with Sage.

Nevertheless the Bar Diamond Bar had allowed Half Circle V to cut hay on Sage Creek for the Williams ranch had plenty of wild native hay on its southern flank on Doggone and Wild Willow and Cottonwood Creeks, streams entering Black Butte River some thirty odd miles below Black Butte town.

Thus his father had allowed Half Circle V to cut Sage Creek's hay. Ric smiled slightly. His thoughts were wasted. Uncle Sam owned Sage Creek except for the homestead taken up by Jim Young.

For a number of years ago some Musselshell Valley cowmen had taken the principle of 'squatter's rights' into the Montana courts. Their basis to claim on a particular piece of land was that they had occupied it first and grazed stock on it.

The state's highest court had upheld the lower courts. The land belonged to Uncle Sam. The cowmen had not homesteaded it.

The verdict had been a big blow to the big cowmen.

And a great boost to the potential homesteader.

Ric glanced at the calendar. He had marked it Church Social for this day. Once a month the church gave a social, the money going to the school.

He'd asked no girl to go with him. He'd been so busy the date had crept up on him.

Who should he ask? Usually he went to the social with Jennie Queen. And if not with Jennie, then with Martha.

He knew that town-gossips awaited anxiously to see which he would marry—Martha or Jennie. He knew both would make good wives and mothers for he wanted at least four children.

Suddenly, he grinned.

He'd skip over both Martha and Jennie. He'd ask Melissa Wentworth to go with him.

He'd seen too much of both Jennie and Martha since coming back from college. Jennie was her usual joking self but it seemed to him that Martha Stewart was becoming a little bossy, too much potential wife, lately.

But would Melissa go with him? She was, after all, a gambler, was she not?

To many Westerners gambling was not an honorable profession. A male gambler was not accepted by some citizens. A female gambler was in many cases completely beyond acceptance.

To Ric Williams, this was pure nonsense. To him gambling was a way to make a living, nothing more or less.

He figured there were honest gamblers just as there were honest lawyers, bankers and other businessmen. Of course, there were dishonest professional and businessmen, too—but that was to be accepted. All classifications in this life held some weaklings.

The theory was that gamblers consorted with prostitutes and others of such nature for gamblers invariably worked in saloons among the whiskey-drinking crowd.

Kitty O'Neill had many chances to put in girls on the second story of her saloon, a thing she never would allow. The upstairs was a respectable hotel usually occupied by drifting cowboys or salesmen.

Ric thought ahead to the social. It would be as dry as desert dust. Since coming back, he'd attended each monthly social. Usually they were held at the schoolhouse or the church, usually the former.

He knew just how things would run. One of the local matrons would have her turn sitting as chairman. She'd call the meeting to order, the secretary would read the minutes, the treasurer make a report. Then matters pertaining to the town would be discussed.

Either Malcolm Stewart or Martha would then give a reading. After this reading, coffee and doghnuts would be served and the meeting adjourned.

Ric admitted to himself he went only because there was nothing more inviting to do that particular night. He enjoyed the company of bouncing Jennie Queen or Martha Stewart.

Were he not to go to the social he'd stay home and read some more pamphlets and he was pretty well filled up with Uncle Sam's words. Last night he'd read about building a reservoir below a check dam to store even more run-off water.

Water then went over a dam's spillway and would enter this big reservoir. Water from the reservoir would go into the head canal. If there was more rain than the dam and the reservoir could hold, this drained out the reservoir spillway.

The reservoir would be built a few feet

above the surface of the earth. It would be long and not very deep. It could be built of concrete and rock. There were plenty of rocks and building sand available along the south hills. His mind glowed with the idea.

He was on the saloon's porch step when Greg Mattson and the Kid came out, heading for their saddle-horses. Neither spoke. They untied, swung up—guns blasting the air. They left town on the dead gallop.

Kitty O'Neill stood in her doorway. Her hands were on her hips and her lips a hard line. "Someday them two will run over some town child an' kill him," she said. "That stuff should be stopped,"

Ric nodded. "I'll bring it up at the social tonight. We're having a general election in August, you know. I'll talk about getting such a stipulation on the ballot then."

"Sheriff Ratchford is gettin' old. He should be retired."

Ric shook his head. "Being pushed to one side would kill him. The way to do it is to hire a deputy sheriff for him and gradually he'll see the light and retire of his own accord."

"That's a good idea, Ric. This town has no mayor. Why not put in a city government and elect a council and mayor? I know a man who'd make a crackerjack of a mayor."

Ric smiled. "Introduce him to me sometime, will you?" Then, seriously he explained that he wanted Miss Melissa Wentworth to accompany him to the social.

Kitty's sharp eyes studied him. "You're wantin' her to accompany you, not me. Don't play the John Alden bit, Ric. It ain't becomin'. Jus' ask her yourself, and see what happens?"

Ric grinned. "I'm not asking you to talk to Melissa for me. I'm merely asking you if you think she'd go—or if she should go."

"You're blushin', Ric Williams!"

Ric's grin widened. "Okay, I'll ask her. Where is she?"

"At her table."

Ric stepped onto the long porch.

"Time this town needs to be waked up," Kitty said. "Some of 'em still look sidewise at me after thirty odd years of runnin' an honorable saloon and hotel."

Ric was lucky. Kitty had only two traveling salesmen at her table. They were playing a low moneyed game just for amusement. The two were waiting for the next stage. They'd taken orders from the few business establishments and were plainly anxious to get out of town and work other small towns, but they were locked here for two more days.

"This town needs rails," one said.

Ric bought a few dollars worth of chips. Melissa smiled at him and Ric liked her smile.

"There'll be rails when more farmers come in," Ric said. "I'm U.S. Land Agent here. The Great Northern has assured me that when there is enough farm and ranch produce to ship out to make it pay the G.N. will run up rails from Malta or a town along the steel."

"Farmers are coming in," one salesman said. "Milk River along G.N. rails is crowded with families looking for homesteads."

"They'll come in," Ric assured.

Kitty came up. She spoke to both salesmen. "You boys are good at figures. I can't balance my books for yesterday. I'd sure be happy to set up a few for the house if you two'd take a look at my scribblin's."

"Certainly, Miss Kitty."

"A pleasure, Kitty."

Kitty winked at Ric. She and the two went into her office. Ric was alone with Melissa. Melissa looked at him.

Ric said, "I want to talk to you."

"I'm here to listen, Ric."

Ric spilled out his invitation. Melissa listened and he detected merriment in her blue-green eyes. He felt like an errant schoolboy admitting he'd stuck the wasp in Sister Maloney's braid.

Melissa said, "I'm a gambler. I was born into a gambling family. My father was Jack Wentworth, and he gambled over the world. My mother was Elizabeth Wentworth, and she ran a table next to my father's."

Ric nodded.

"I was teethed on a poker chip. I know what's bothering you. Will I be accepted at this social? That's your problem."

Ric opened his mouth to speak, but a gesture silenced him.

"You're a good man, Richard Williams. I know that you're not thinking of yourself —that if I accompany you, you'll not be lowering your local social standing. You're thinking of me. You don't want me embarrassed."

Ric nodded.

"Well, I'm Melissa Wentworth. I'm twenty-two and never been married. If you want to know the truth, for what it is worth, I'm still a virgin—waiting for the right man."

She blushed not a bit, Ric noticed. His estimation of her went upwards.

He wisely kept silent.

"Someday I'll find that man. I want a handful of children with him. I want to be a wife and mother. I'm telling you too much, maybe?"

"No, no! Definitely not! Go on, please!"

"Before I came here I had a poker table across the river from El Paso, Texas—in Juarez, Chihuahua, old Mexico, to be exact. Rich Texans came over to gamble because Texas has so many blue-sky laws."

Ric listened.

"One day I looked over the crowd and my stomach crawled. I cashed in my chips, walked across the International Bridge to El Paso, and got the first train north—and here I am."

"How do you like it here?"

Melissa Wentworth's eyes glowed. "I love it here. Every moment, every hour, every day—I'm a smalltown girl at heart, I've discovered. I'm going to homestead here—so you save me a good homestead, eh?"

"That I sure will. How about tonight's social?"

"You and I, Richard Williams!"

VII

EARLY NEXT morning Ric Williams stood behind Greg Mattson's horse-barn talking to Mattson. Kid Hannigan was in the background, listening.

Ric explained. "Here is the section marker. It's forty feet from this barn's southeast corner and the section line."

Mattson listened.

"Now if you run your east homestead line straight north all your buildings will fall inside your homestead's limits except that stone building there."

Greg Mattson looked at the offending building. It was twenty feet by twenty, made of stone and concrete, and his father had had it built as a powderhouse, for Scott Mattson had dynamited stumps from the river bank to make a horse pasture, years and years ago.

"What if I run my east homestead boundary south?" Greg Mattson asked.

Ric grinned. "You'll have only one of

your buildings inside your homestead, and that would be that little stone building."

"An' my other buildin's—? The house, barns, corrals, all thet—it would be on government land? Anybody could file on the lan'—an' own my buildings then?"

"That's right."

Greg Mattson frowned. "Couldn't you stretch the limits a bit south to take in this powderhouse? I'll make it worth your while, Ric."

Ric said shortly. "You trying to bribe me, Mattson?" His voice had taken on hardness.

"Call it what you want, Williams. But I'll make it worth your while if you extend the limits far enough south to include this building."

Ric said, "I could report you to Uncle Sam. He'd bring up a charge of attempting to bribe a U.S. official."

"Who'd be your witness?"

Ric looked at Kid Hannigan.

The gunman laughed. "I'm like the three monkeys. I see nothin', hear nothin', say nothin'."

Ric spoke to Mattson. "There is a way to get control of the powderhouse, though."

"Name it."

"You could run your homestead south

and hope your father homesteaded the area north, where your buildings are."

"No go on that. What if the ol' man never homesteaded? By doin' that I'd gain this shack an' lose all the rest."

Ric nodded.

Mattson had made up his mind. "Run your lines aroun' my main buildin's. An' if the ol' man had already homesteaded them, my entry would automatically be null an' void, wouldn't it?"

"It would," Ric assured. "No two can land on the same homestead. If this happens, the one filing first has priority."

"That college learned you a hell of a lot of big words," Greg Mattson said. "Maybeso in time you'll start talkin' so people can understan' you ag'in?"

Ric let that ride with, "Perhaps. . . ."

Greg Mattson said, "You help the man, Hannigan," and turned away and Ric said, "My fee for running lines is fifty dollars in advance, Mattson."

Mattson stopped, turned. "You don't trust me?"

"Uncle Sam's orders, not mine."

"You seem handy in turnin' the blame onto the federal gover'ment, not on yourself. What if I don't have fifty smackers on me?"

"Then your homestead entry is automatically null and void," Ric said.

Greg Mattson took out his wallet. He threw gold pieces toward Ric. Sunlight glistened on the yellow metal. Ric saw two double eagles and an eagle land beside a sagebrush.

"You got a receipt coming," Ric pointed out.

"Give it to Hannigan."

Mattson went around the barn's corner. Ric picked up the money, anger burning. He spoke to Kid Hannigan. "I've already paced off the homestead's limits running north. We'll walk around them and I'll show you my stakes."

"One hundred and sixty acres?"

"That's right. A half-mile square."

"An' we walk that distance?" the gunman asked.

"Why not?"

"That's two miles, on the hoof."

Ric grinned. "I wanted you to walk it so you'd know exactly where the fence will go, but you can ride out and find the markers. I'll write you a receipt for the fifty bucks. You can ride the line or not. Makes no never-mind to me. I'm not anxious for your company, anyway."

Kid Hannigan had his hand on his holstered weapon. "Watch your tongue, lawyer!"

Ric laughed. "At least you called me lawyer and not shyster! My reputation must be picking up." He took a notebook from his shirt pocket and scrawled a receipt. "Here it is for your Nibs," he said, and swung up on his big bay gelding, Snorty.

Snorty carried quite a load besides his master for Ric had his tripod and measuring rod tied to the saddle, also. Wry disgust pulled at the land locator's innards. The day had not started out good. Then he remembered last night . . . and Melissa Wentworth.

To his surprise, Melissa had been quickly accepted. Her gracious manners and courtesy immediately registered with the men and while some older women grudgingly gave in the younger were soon in accord.

Malcolm Stewart or Martha did not give the customary reading. Melissa was called upon. Ric discovered she'd been in some Shakespeare plays while in high school.

She gave part of Macbeth. Ric listened in surprise, wishing he'd paid more attention to Macbeth in college. When she'd finished, Ric had watched the audience.

Men had applauded heartily. Some of the older women—church goers—gave what seemed grudging recommendation. The younger people—both male and female—also gave full applause.

During the lunch period Martha and Jennie Queen chatted with Melissa, who apparently had visited foreign countries. Others of the young people—both male and female—listened. Melissa became elated and happy. While walking home she held onto Ric's arm, and Ric liked that.

"I'm sure happy you invited me, Ric."

"You were great," Ric said. "Have a good time?"

"Wonderful."

They parted on the steps of the saloon. Except for a light or two upstairs the saloon was dark—for Kitty O'Neill closed early most week nights for lack of customers. As saloons went, her saloon was not the biggest money-maker around. A sort of family bar, she called it.

The night was calm. There was no moon but stars were dazzling bright in the cloudless Montana sky. She stood on the top step above Ric and therefore was a bit taller than he.

She called gently upstairs, "Kitty, darling."

"Comin' down, Melissa."

Melissa spoke to Ric. "Miss Kitty is like a mother to me. My mama died three years ago—the same time papa died—Cholera in Hong Kong. I was in college, in Texas."

"She's very nice," Ric said, and meant it. His mother and father had thought the world of Miss Kitty O'Neill, who many times had visited Bar Diamond Bar when Brent and Augusta Williams had been living.

Ric heard Kitty unlock the big front doors. Melissa said softly, "Thanks again, Ric," and she kissed him lightly on the cheek and ran to the door and disappeared inside, her voice and Kitty's momentarily coming back.

Ric had walked home on clouds. He then remembered that both Jennie Queen and Martha Stewart had at times kissed him and his boots had gone down this lonesome dark street again on anything but solid soil.

Riding down on Hell Creek, he wished he'd had a talk with Greg—a serious conversation—about the fact that Greg said he was losing cattle to rustlers.

But he hadn't had time. The occasion had not arisen. All the time the sword's point came through, separating him and Greg Mattson. Ric Williams sighed. Why in the hell did two persons always have to hate each other?

He didn't like the word *hate*. He didn't hate Greg Mattson. He changed from *hate* to *dislike*.

Snorty went down-slope, forelegs stiff, hind legs sliding, the surveying equipment bobbing, and while coming down hill, Ric looked over the farms—if such they could be called—of George Hess, Jake Mullins and Ward Griffin, his first three clients.

All three had strung up three strands of barbwire around their quarter sections. Their farms were located on the meadowlands that Hell Creek—now tame and sluggish—inhabited.

Ric watered Snorty on Hell Creek. He looked about. Cottonwoods and boxelders were green and gave shade. Yonder had been a clump of diamond willows. An axe had cut out all the willows big enough to make posts. One of the farmers had done that cutting.

Overhead a chicken-hawk circled. Magpies chirped in the trees. Ric had little respect for the gaudy black and white bird with his sharp, long beak. Magpies were nest robbers.

He remembered his favorite boyhood swimming hole miles south of Hangman's Creek. There a pair of owls had made a nest of many twigs in the tip of a cottonwood tree.

He'd climbed up and looked at the eggs. They'd appeared very small to be eggs of big owls. He kept an eye on the eggs. Finally they hatched but the nest held not young owls but young magpies.

Magpies had eaten the owl's eggs when the nest had momentarily been vacated. The mother owl had sat patiently on magpie eggs, not knowing the difference. She then tried to raise a family of magpies. How she came out on the deal Ric never knew for one day the nest was empty and no owls or magpies were in evidence.

Snorty lifted his head, sniffed the air, then pricked his ears north, and Ric saw one of his farmers, George Hess, come out of the brush and head in his direction, Winchester rifle in hand.

"Still hunting a buck?" Ric asked.

"Well, I'm shootin' to kill at a deer—buck only—if I happen to run acrost such, but us three after thet trouble Young had in town has been kinda keepin' up a guard, night an' day, Ric."

"Half Circle V?"

"That's right. We've seen a few riders in the distance. Couldn't tell who they was, but they might've been Mattson hands."

"And they could have been somebody else, too."

Slow-speaking Hess asked, "Like who, mebbe?"

"Cow thieves. Rustlers."

"You believe really that Mattson's lost cattle in the dead of winter to cow-thieves?"

"I have no reason to doubt his word."

Hess considered that for some moments. "You know him better'n I do. I've done heered you an' him has had dozens of fistfights, ever since in the first grade—so I reckon you know him better than me."

"I've always found Greg Mattson honest." Ric smiled. "and with hard fists, too." He touched a scar over his right eye significantly.

"They say he had cowboys take tallies on the dead cattle they found on roundup a few weeks back. A count like thet in my opinion couldn't be anyway correct, Ric."

"Why do you say that?"

"First, some would be killed by wolves an' c'yotes. Then when the snow melted the run-off water was bound to wash some of the carcasses into the river and away they'd go—sink down or float off."

"You got a point there. I'll say the same about wolves and coyotes, but this spring the snow melted very, very slow—and there was very little run-off water."

"That's right. Lookin' back now I cain't remember Hell Crick gettin' but a few feet above normal when the snow melted. Now who in the name of hell would be rustlin' cows in the dead of cold winter?"

Ric tried being blunt. "He suspects you an' Mullins an' Griffin."

"Us—farmers?"

Hess' voice held a note of surprise. Ric wondered whether it was genuine or feigned. Hess was no fool. Neither were Mullins or Griffin. Surely they must have guessed they were under Half Circle V's suspicion?

"You sound as though that thought is new to you, Hess."

Hess gave this some consideration. "No, can't say it is. Me an' Mullins an' Griffin have talked it over, since hearin' Mattson make that statement—but we weren't sure although we figured so."

"Where are Griffin and Mullins now?"

"Mullins' seedin' corn. Griffin is seedin' wheat. I got most of my twenty acres in afore the rain. Got it in barley. Comin' up nice. Plowin' as much more as I can afore the dry comes again an' makes plowin' impossible."

"Where's your bronc?"

"Home. I'm on foot."

Ric kicked a boot from left stirrup. "Swing up behind me, Hess."

"This horse carry double without bucking?"

"He carries double okay."

Hess put his brogan in the stirrup. Soon he was mounted behind Ric's cantle, Snorty carrying double. Snorty crossed Hell Creek in the riffles where there was a rock bottom.

The horse and his two riders came out of the brush. Here were the three farms of the three original farmers. Barbwire shimmered under the hot sun.

Each farmer had built a dug-out back

into a hill. These had been warmer during the past hard winter than any frame or sod or log shack would have been. The dugouts did not sport wooden doors. Each doorframe was covered by a thick canvas.

Ward Griffin's farm was first. Griffin was walking with a hand-seeder blowing out wheat kernels. He mopped his brow. "Glad you came along, Ric. Gave me a reason to stop workin' in this damn' hot sun."

Ric looked north. The next homestead belonged to Jake Mullins. Mullins had hoed up rows. He now walked along with a stick poking holes in the top of the ridges.

Into each hole, he dropped a kernel of corn. As he went to the next hole his big foot flattened the area he'd just planted.

Griffin cupped his hands to his mouth, his cry ringing across the prairie. Mullins stopped working. Griffin waved. Mullins started in their direction.

"Howdy, men. Howdy, Mr. Williams. Ain't nothin' gone haywire now, has they?" Mullins asked.

"We four need to have a pow-wow," Ric said.

VIII

AFTER CONFABBING with the Hell Creek farmers Ric Williams reined Snorty south toward Sage Creek, the black bulk of Black Butte to his left, silent guardian over this wilderness area.

Six miles of bench-land lay between Hell Creek and the new farmers on Sage Creek. Sometimes the land was flat and then again it was marred by coulees and deep draws.

Rain had turned this region very green. Ric figured this land would never be farmed. Its contours were too rough and because of its elevation it could not be irrigated.

Ric had read all he could find on dry-land farming. Dry-land farming meant you farmed without irrigation. Government reports showed that this area had about twelve inches of rain a year on the average.

And this rain did not come at a particular time as rain did in Minnesota and North Dakota to the east. Rain here came whenever it felt like it and not on specific times.

For head crops such as wheat, corn, barley and oats needed one good soaking just after the seed had been planted. This sprouted the seed and brought up the plant.

Corn was completely eliminated here. It needed rain after rain, but the other head crops needed just one more rain after being sprouted. This rain should come when the plants were forming kernels.

Then warm weather should occur, filling the heads and hardening the grain for the harvest.

Ric figured this bench-land was very valuable, though—at least, in his plans—for he intended to farm after settling other farmers. And on this bench-land he'd graze his fullblooded Shorthorn cattle, for he guessed this bench-land would never be taken up as homesteads.

He would not raise cattle in the thousands as had his father and Scott Mattson. At the most, he'd never have over five hundred head, he figured.

And these would not be bony longhorned, hard-beefed Longhorns. They'd be gentle, beef-to-the-hocks cattle. Each steer would have at least four times the beef a longhorn steer of the same age packed.

And it wouldn't be stringy, tough beef.

The steaks would be tender and juicy. And the Shorthorn beef wouldn't draw the lowest prices per hundred weight on the market. It would pull down the highest.

There'd be no beeves of his wandering gaunt and cold before blizzards. His prize cattle would be behind windbreaks or in barns when blizzards howled. They'd be dining on green alfalfa taken from one of the stacks his irrigated fields had raised.

And springs and summer these cattle would graze on these bench-lands. Maybeso by that time Uncle Sam would charge a grazing fee per head but he felt sure that fee would not be high—if, indeed, such eventually would be fixed.

He was anxious to get on with his work. He'd put hands to work building check dams soon. Again he silently thanked his dead father for the money Brent Williams had left behind.

He'd build old Bar Diamond Bar into new Bar Diamond Bar. His pureblooded stock would become well-known across Montana. His young bulls would sell for a small fortune. . . .

He was brought down to earth by Snorty stumbling. Looking back, Ric saw the exposed root of a big cottonwood tree. The bronc had dragged a front shoe over this.

Ric Williams breathed deeply of the good air, recognizing that only one real dark cloud lay over this land—and that was the fact that Half Circle V was losing cattle.

Apparently cow-thieves were at work here on Black Butte range. He accepted Greg Mattson's words.

Before progress could be achieved the rustlers had to be ferreted out and eliminated, he knew. This basin could not prosper with thieves in the midst of its honest folk.

He'd pointed this out to his three Hell Creek farmers. He'd been blunt and to the point.

"All I know about you three is what I have seen and heard since I settled you on your homesteads. I don't know where you came from, what your past life has been —and frankly, gentlemen, I don't give a damn."

The three had listened in silence.

"I do know none of you has had a criminal record. Had you had such, it would have turned up on the final study made into your eligibility to homestead."

A hawk soared silently overhead.

"But Mattson has been losing cattle. I can't say Greg Mattson and I are the world's closest friends but I've never found him or his father or mother to be anything but truthful. So if Mattson says he's been losing stock, Mattson has had his herds rustled."

"Don't look t'me," Hess said.

"Me, either," Mullins informed.

Griffin said, "I'm no cowthief."

Ric had held up his hands in silence. "I'm accusing nobody. But common sense and logic must tell you that you're under suspicion."

"Suspicion's wasted," Hess said shortly.

"But just the same it's there," Ric said.

Griffin asked, "What's the point, Williams?"

Irritation held the farmers. Ric chose his next words with deliberate care.

"I don't know how much cash each of you have. I don't care to know, either. But don't flash money around, please. By having a few a bucks suspicion would grow stronger towards you."

The three knew full well what he meant. Cowstealing was a capital offense in this primitive land. They hanged cow-thieves fast and without a trial. The same held for horse-stealing.

"Black Butte's citizens look peaceful but when aroused they're a tough bunch. A few years ago a traveling salesman got a little fresh with one of the bigger girls. The town tarred and feathered him and rode him out of town on a rail to leave him on the prairie naked except for the tar and the feathers."

"I've heard about that," Griffin said.

"My father and our cowpunchers went out and picked the man up in a buggy and took him to our ranch where they cleaned him up and put clean clothes over the big sores the hot tar had made. They took him to Malta and he had a tough time in the hospital there but he lived through it."

"And he never harmed the girl, so I heard," Hess said.

"Never harmed her," Ric repeated. "Well, gentlemen, I guess that's all I've got to say."

"Thanks for the warnin'," Mullins said.

"We're still postin' a man on guard, night an' day," Hess said.

Ric nodded. "Your business, gentlemen."

He was surprised to meet Sheriff Ratchford two miles south on the bench-land. The heavy-set sheriff sat saddle on a big gray gelding.

Ratchford came out of a coulee. Ric had

the feeling the sheriff had been watching him from concealment in the brush.

"Looking for me, sheriff?" Ric joked.

"Mebbe. Mebbeso not. You stole any Half Circle V cows lately?"

"Just shipped a mite more than a hundred head out on the Canadian Pacific up north," Ric joked. "Cow-buyer bought them up in Timber Mountain north of the Line."

"You don't say."

"Cash deal, too. Money's in my saddlebag. Off side one." Ric became serious. "Out scouting, sheriff?"

"Right, Ric."

Ric told of the lecture he'd just given his three Hell Creek farmers.

"How'd they take it?" Sheriff Ratchford asked.

Ric shrugged. "In their stride, a man might say. I wonder if Greg Mattson's lost any head since calf-branding roundup?"

"He says he has. Had a marker over on Wisdom Hill. Roan steer with a knocked-down off-side horn. Greg says the steer is gone. Scoured that range good, but no roan steer."

Ric nodded seriously.

"Lost another marker north of Black Butte about ten miles. Steer with a throw in his off front hoof. Born with the thing, Greg told me—somethin' like a baby born with a club foot, you might say."

"Cripple, eh? Could he travel fast enough to be run off, you figure?"

"Greg said he got along as good as a steer without the throw. And he tol' me he an' some of his hands worked that section for ten miles each way—and no club-footed steer."

"Where does Mattson think his range has less head than it should have, sheriff?"

Sheriff Ratchford rubbed his whiskery jaw. Snorty played with the cricket in his spade bit, making a musical sound—a habit Snorty had.

"From his complaint, I'd figger the north end has less than it should carry. The cattle runnin' south aroun' your father's ol' range hasn't been touched as much as the northern herds, Greg thinks."

Ric nodded thoughtfully.

"Since farmers has moved in all over eastern Montana the Stockman's Association has sure tightened its belt against cow-thieves. Got three special agents workin' with the Malta sheriff's office alone, checkin' meat sold along the railroad down south." The sheriff spat on a sagebrush.

A horsefly landed on Snorty's shoulder. Ric made a swipe at it but missed.

"Seems odd, Greg hasn't called in a Stockman's detective," Ric said. "His father and mine were charter members of the Association. He's one of Montana's biggest cowmen."

"I asked him about this. He said this was his business an' not the Association's. I asked him what he meant by that. He jus' looked at me an' said for me to draw my own conclusions."

Ric nodded. "I've been wondering why he hasn't moved against my farmers, but that ruckus Young had with Hannigan is the only trouble he and my farmers have had—except a few fistfights between his men and my three Hell Creek farmers in Kitty's saloon."

"An' Greg wasn't involved in any of them fights. Only thing thet caused them was thet the farmers were drunk an' so were a couple of Half Circle V cowpunchers, too."

"How come he's holding back, sheriff?"

"I asked him that. He said he'd let the farmers raise their head-crops up high enough to amount to cow-feed an' then he'd move his hands in an' take over."

"That'd mean gun-play," Ric said.

"I mentioned that mebbeso there wouldn't be enough rain to raise crops. We jus' had a good rain but one rain don't make a wheat field. He said he figured that the farmers couldn't stay—this was no farmin' land, he said. So he said he'd wait and see."

"Sensible thinking," Ric said.

"Main point of argument is them grass meadows on Sage an' Hell Cricks. Half Circle V mowers has cut grass there for years. Enough farmers moved in on them cricks an' take over Mattson hay then I think all hell might bust loose, Ric."

"I wrote Maresh in Malta. Asked him to send in no more farmers until this trouble is settled. Fact is, he might notify Uncle Sam and Uncle might send the black troops from Fort Assiniboine to hold down peace."

"He might, at that."

"This is like sitting on a volcano," Ric said. "Man never knows at what moment it might erupt and hit him in the rump with red-hot lava."

"The whole county is on edge, Ric. The kids in town don't play Cowboy an' Injun no more. They play Half Circle V an' sodbusters. Unless this is settled soon— an' danged soon—the whole range will be reachin' for guns."

"Rustled cattle," Ric said.

"Me, I figger them stolen cows is one of the big blocks holdin' up this thing. With that solved, Mattson will see things clearer. I'm sure—but this rustlin' has got to stop."

Ric said, "I figure Mattson thinks for sure those three farmers I moved in last fall are doing the stealing."

"An' as you said, the farmers say Greg is full of hot air, eh?"

"That's what they told me."

The lawman sighed. "But that's how trouble starts—differences in opinion. Millions of men have been killed in battle over less." He shifted in stirrups. "Mind if I ride along with you to see how them new farmers are?"

"I'd welcome it, sheriff."

The three new farmers were okay. They were dead drunk along with their old buddy, Jim Young. The three loaded wagons stood before Young's crude habitation, horses out on Young's pasture. Rogers and Winston had drunk themselves to insensibility.

They slept in the shade next to Young's shack, snoring in drunken sleep. Smith Jones and Jim Young sat in the shade, backs to the shack's wall, and sipped from a bottle of Old Shoe, then took a drink of spring water as a chaser. Both were about ready to capsize, Ric judged.

Young tried to get to his boots as Ric and Sheriff Ratchford rode in. He couldn't quite make it. He sank down again saying, "Light an' rest your saddles, men. Have a cup or two with ol' friends."

He slurred his words. Ric smiled. Smith Jones didn't even try to rise. He sat there with legs spread out and said, "Rich and Williams, eh? Yes, an' the barber from Black Butte."

Young poked Smith with his elbow. "Barbers don't wear law stars, you damn' fool. That's Sheriff Rachman."

The sheriff grinned at Ric. "Ratchford, not Rachman," he corrected.

"Sorry," Young said. "Take a drink, men. Spring water as a chaser. Whiskey first, then water."

Ric and the sheriff dismounted, gear creaking. Smith got to his feet with trouble and said, "I'll take your horses to the creek and water them," and Ric said, "Sit down, Smith. We watered our horses as we rode in."

Smith sank down again and reached for the bottle. He handed it to Ric who took a long swallow and handed the Old Shoe to

Sheriff Ratchford, who raised it and merely wet his lips.

Ric's belly burned. He realized quite a few hours had passed since he'd cooked his early-morning breakfast. He killed the fire with spring water, thinking that one more big shot of this would send him looplegged, also.

He handed the water jug to the sheriff, who drank.

"How come you ride out all this way from town, Mr. Williams?" Smith Jones asked.

"Ain't but five, six miles into town," Jim Young told Smith Jones.

"Seemed longer when we druv out yesterday," the new farmer said. "Reckon it seemed long because we was in a hurry to join our friends again."

"Thanks for the nice compliment," Jim Young said. "Have a drink on me, Smith?"

"Don't mind if I do," Smith Jones said, and drank.

Ric spoke to Young. "Haven't had any trouble, have you?"

"Trouble? With who?"

"Half Circle V."

"Couple of Mattson's men rode by this morning early. I went out with my rifle an' talked to them. They'd been sent out by their boss to see how long the bluejoint grass was on the Meadows, no more."

"Nothin' else?" Sheriff Ratchford asked.

Jim Young put blood-shot eyes on the lawman. "Should there have been anythin' else?" His voice held the belligerency of a drunk.

"Not a thing more," the sheriff hurriedly said. Without Young or Jones noticing, he inclined his head slightly—indicating to Ric they should go, and Ric turned Snorty east toward Black Butte.

"I rode out to establish section lines with you boys," he said, "but that can wait, seeing you're all busy."

"I got their homesteads staked out," Jim Young said. "Did it in my spare time from thet map you gave me, Mr. Williams."

"I'll be back some other day," Ric said.

He and the sheriff loped toward Black Butte. The sun was hot and already bits of dust lifted behind hoofs, even after such a long and soaking rain. Ric shifted weight on stirrups.

He looked northeast toward high Black Butte. Between his location and Black Butte was a long and low bench-land running east and west and ending on the west bank of Black Butte River.

This ridge was spiked with pine and buckbrush and occasional big sandstone boulders. When a boy he'd ridden his pony onto this rimrock and spent the afternoon hunting cottontail rabbits with his single-shot Marlin .22 rifle.

Cottontails abounded there. They lived in dens dug out under the sandstones. Once he'd shot a bobcat whom he'd surprised hunting cottontails. His small .22 lead had not killed the cat immediately.

He'd trailed the wounded animal by the bloodspots and had found it dead in the brush. He'd skinned it and taken the pelt home and the old foreman, Luther Brush, had shown him how to tan the hide.

The bobcat's tanned pelt still lay on the floor of his boyhood room in the old ranch-house.

Quite by accident, he caught a flash reflection in one group of sandstones. He kept his eyes on the spot but didn't catch another. He told Sheriff Ratchford, "That big bunch of sandstones there. Straight north, almost."

"What about them?"

He told of the reflection. "Looked to me

like the sun slanting off the glass of a pair of field-glasses, maybe. Anyway, somebody up there is watching us, sheriff."

"Kid Hannigan."

Ric looked at the sheriff. "Why the Kid?"

"My field glasses picked him up just afore I ran into you, Ric. You didn't know it but apparently he was trailin' you."

"Trailing me? I wonder why?"

"Reckon Greg Mattson wanted to know where you were going. Or mebbeso the Kid wanted to know, an' mebbeso he went of his own accord—not because his boss ordered him."

"I don't cotton to the Kid."

"Lotsa others don't, either. For one thing, they says he's a gunman an' Greg hired him not to punch cows, but ride gun-guard over him. That's something completely new on this range."

Ric nodded.

"Then they remember he come in about the same time them three cowpuncher farmers of yours settled on Hell Crick. An' right after that Greg Mattson complained to me he was losin' stock."

"Doesn't look good," Ric said.

"Not good at all," the sheriff said.

IX

Ric Williams ate supper with Martha Stewart in the Longhorn Cafe. Usually he and Martha chatted and joked but this evening he was silent most of the time and Martha asked, "Something on the lawyer's mind?"

"Only my hat."

"You don't even wear your hat. It's hung on the hatrack over there."

"For once, I'm thinking."

"About what?"

"Lots of things. You know, this town seems to be sitting on a powderkeg, with a slow fuse burning."

"Did you notice that, too? Daddy said the same at dinner this noon. It's all because of you and Greg Mattson."

"Thank you."

"No, that's the truth, Ric. You're moving in farmers. They're squatting on hayland Greg claims. And then Greg says that since you moved those three farmers on Hell Creek he's lost cattle."

"I wonder if he really has."

"Why would he say different?"

"To promote trouble—more trouble—between him and my farmers. And with me, of course. Push things to a climax faster."

Martha thoughtfully cut her steak. "Well, I see that point of view—Yes, that's possible. But I know Greg—We both went to grammar school together. Frankly, I don't think he has such a devious mind—a mind that could conceive such a situation—Or am I wrong?"

"You're not wrong. I think he's more straightforward, as you say—and he'd have a hard time thinking up such a situation."

"Let's talk about something else, eh?"

"Such as what?"

Ric shrugged. "You got me."

Ric sensed an unspoken barrier between himself and this pretty brown haired teacher. This was something new. It had not been there until he'd escorted Melissa Wentworth to the social.

Later on that evening he visited the Queen home. Jennie was talkative and her usual self—or so it would have seemed to an outsider, but Ric also sensed a wall between him and this lovely woman—something that had not been there before the social.

Now he knew how a husband felt when his wife caught him kissing her sister. He grinned to himself and they finished their game of whist and Jennie said, "I baked a cake today."

They were alone in the Queen dining room. Her mother had retired to her room to read and her father had returned to the Merc to work on his monthly balance sheet.

"With coffee, Ric."

Ric was at the point of begging off but pushed it aside, for Jennie was indeed a wonderful young woman and common gossip said the man who got her would have a wonderful wife—but gossip said the same about Martha Stewart, also.

Ric left full of cake and coffee and a nice big kiss from Jennie who had stood on the porch floor with Ric on the step below and had repeated what Martha had done just a couple of hours before.

Ric didn't quite understand why he'd made these two social calls. He had the impression he was saying goodbye to the two girls. It was a loco sensation and was groundless and he blamed it on one of those whims a man gets and brings about . . . for no apparent reason.

He started for home, then stopped. He looked up street toward Kitty O'Neill's saloon. Two lights were upstairs. That meant two customers for her hotel. The saloon was lighted, too—but it looked as though not all the kerosene lamps were lighted.

Kitty lit all the lamps only when she had customers. This was a week day and far from any payday so with such a dim light inside Ric figured the saloon had few customers.

His logic proved correct. Sheriff Ratchford and another old-timer stood at the bar drinking beer, the bar's only two customers. A drunken cowboy slept on the pool table.

Ric noticed the cowpuncher wore no boots. Somebody had pulled off his boots and spurs so he'd not make holes on the pool table's expensive cloth.

Kitty had many times told him spurs and pool tables didn't mix. He glanced at Melissa's table.

There were three poker tables. Melissa was the only gambler, though. And none of the tables was occupied.

His heart fell. Melissa evidently was upstairs in her room. For some reason he wouldn't admit to himself he wanted to see the blonde woman again.

Sheriff Ratchford called, "Have a beer with me an' Slim, Ric boy?"

"Don't care if I do," Ric said.

The bartender dozed on his high chair. Ric reached over the bar, speared a bottle of Great Falls Brew, uncorked it with corkscrew on his jackknife, and lifted the bottle, eyes on the stairway.

His heart jumped. Melissa was coming down the stairs. She wore a long black dress with a white jabot and her hair was done in a nice blonde bun behind her pretty neck.

She came to his elbow. "I heard you men talking upstairs and I heard your name called, Ric." She smiled prettily. "No trade tonight—and I was sitting alone, tired of reading—"

She did not drink, even beer. Black Butte town had learned that—to its surprise—in a short time. A woman who worked in a saloon—a gambling woman—and she didn't drink?

Was it possible?

"Let's sit down and talk," Ric said.

"Let's go outside on the porch. How are the mosquitoes tonight?"

"Enough wind to drive them off."

Ric killed his beer and then followed her delightfully small waist out onto the porch, where they sat on the top step, Black Butte town running south before them, all two blocks of it.

"Not many lights in houses," Melissa said.

"Folks here go to bed early. They get up early."

Melissa said, "I haven't seen you all day."

Ric gave an account of his day. He felt happy that someone cared enough about him to ask what he'd done this day. To his surprise she told him she'd rented a small building and was starting a saddle and harness shop.

Ric scowled. "You know anything about saddles? Or harnesses?"

Melissa laughed. "Only that they're made out of leather! But a salesman who spent a day here—Mr. Hans Christenson—said he knew a young man who is an apprentice to Koke down in Malta and this young man wants to start a saddle shop—leather shop, that is—And I got some money to spare. And besides, I never was cut out to be a gambler."

Ric knew Koke. Koke built some of Montana's strongest and best saddles. The last time in Malta he'd bought a new latigo strap and he'd talked to Koke, who said he was very busy—and not repairing saddles, but repairing harnesses for the new settlers.

"When you get in lots of farmers, my shop will be very busy, I'm sure. What do you think of my plan, Ric?"

Ric caught her two hands. He held them. She made no effort to free them. "I think it's wonderful. I know that apprentice, too. His name is Sam Hoffard."

"That's the name. I should have him—or a letter from him—on tomorrow's stage."

"He'll come. I know him well. He went to school here a couple of years. I was in the seventh and eighth grades and he was in the second, or third, I don't remember which."

"Oh, that's nice."

"I talked to him the last time I was in Malta. He asked me if this town had a saddle and harness shop."

"So far the Merc has been selling saddles and things saddles need, I understand."

"Yes, but to repair a saddle, they sent it out. And I daresay the Merc hasn't a harness in stock."

"I asked. They haven't."

Ric grudgingly released her hands. "Congratulations, Melissa."

"I'm so happy. I know I'll make a success."

"Were you a drinking woman, I'd drink to you on that."

"Your bottle is empty. Don't hesitate about drinking another because I don't drink."

"You don't even drink a beer now and then?"

She shook her blonde head. "I'm not a prude. Others can have a drink if they want to. That's their business. But I've seen what alcohol can do . . . if carried to a great degree."

"Nobody could make a drunk out of me," Ric said. "Only beer, and then not much of that—it makes me sick. I had to take a shot of hard stuff out at my farmers' this afternoon. I can still staste it."

They talked for another hour, occasionally batting at a wayward mosquito, and then Ric went to his bachelor quarters. He slept there. He was up and dressed before dawn and he rode out of Black Butte town when it was still dark . . . and he fell out of circulation for around two weeks.

Sheriff Ike Ratchford noticed that Ric's land-office was closed the next day. He picked up Ric's mail when the northbound stage finally rocked in. The stage carried one salesman and a tall young man whom the sheriff vaguely recognized—or thought he did.

"Could I ask you your name, young man? I'm Sheriff Ike Ratchford."

"You don't remember me?"

"I do, and then I don't."

"I'm Sam Hoffard."

"Son of Minnie an' Ralph Hoffard?"

"That's right."

"Oh, I remember now. You went to school here some years gone an' then your folks moved to Malta. How's your father and your good mother?"

"Both fine, sir. Thank you, sir."

Sheriff Ike Ratchford tried Ric's door. It was locked. He shoved the letters under the door.

He'd noticed one was from Mr. Clarence Maresh, U.S. Land Agent, from Malta. He remembered Ric saying he'd written his boss asking him to send in no more farmers until this damn' trouble was over . . . if it ever would be.

Maresh had evidently received Ric's letter. This letter was Ric's reply. No more farmers had driven in. Maresh evidently was holding them back. So far, so good, the sheriff thought.

The lawman figured Ric had ridden out early, evidently checking on the whereabouts of the three Hell Creek farmers. To make sure, he walked back into the alley.

Snorty wasn't in Ric's barn.

He came back on Main Street. Miss Melissa Wentworth and Ralph Hoffard came out of the saloon. They came downstreet half a block and then Miss Wentworth unlocked the door of the small building the other side of the Gunther drugstore and both entered.

Sheriff Ike Ratchford scowled. That little building had been vacant for some years. Sometimes the Merc stored things there when the Merc's warehouse got too full but he couldn't remember the building being used even for that purpose for quite a long time.

The building belonged to the Widder Matthews who had long tried to rent it out but couldn't because nothing happened in town that would require a store or any establishment.

Sheriff Ratchford had a long nose. He had learned over the years that it paid him to be inquisitive. He'd learned a lot by curiosity—some that had helped him in his law duties.

Accordingly, he made it a point to pass the old building. The building had two front windows, one on each side of the door. Both windows were wide open. He figured they were open because somebody wanted to ventilate the building's insides.

The door was open, too. He looked in. Melissa and young Hoffard had brooms and were sweeping cobwebs from corners and ceiling.

"Cleanin' the joint out, eh?" the sheriff said.

Melissa stopped sweeping. "I'm opening a saddle and harness shop here," she said, "Mr. Hoffard here is working for me. He'll be the man who does the sewing and riveting."

"Sheriff Ratchford remembers me from the days I lived here," Ralph Hoffard told Melissa.

"Harnesses, too? Along with saddles?" the sheriff asked.

"With farmers coming in, there'll be a lot of harness work," Melissa said. "Mr. Hoffard is renting a horse and riding back to Malta with a check on my account there. He'll buy the sewing machines—"

"More than one machine?" the sheriff asked.

"A machine for me, too," Melissa said. "I can learn to sew leather, I'm sure."

"I'll teach you," young Hoffard said.

"By golly," the sheriff said, "I'll wager inside a month you'll be buildin' saddles, Miss Wentworth. You're a woman who when she makes up her mind can do whatever she wants. I'd hate to be the man you'd set yourself to marry. He wouldn't have a chance to escape—" Sheriff Ike Ratchford looked at her blonde beauty. "I take thet back, here an' now—I'd cotton to be the man you'd hunt down to marry."

"You got company," young Hoffard said.

Melissa Wentworth said, "Thank you, kind sirs." She leaned on her broom and looked about. "Guess we got them all out, Mr. Hoffard—the spiders and cobwebs, I mean. I wonder if Ric has another horse besides Snorty—one I could hire to have Mr. Hoffard ride back to Malta?"

"Ric ain't in town," the sheriff said.

"Oh . . . We had a nice talk last night on the porch steps and he never mentioned leaving town today."

"Snorty's gone," the sheriff explained. "An' he don't have no other cayuse. Kitty's got some horses eatin' their fool heads off in the town livery, or didn't you know that, Miss Wentworth?"

"I know that, sir. But I dislike asking her to lend us one, she's been so good to me—"

"Shaw, she'll be offended if you don't ask. Could I spread the word aroun' about your new establishment?"

"You sure can. We'll be in business in about a week. Is that right, Mr. Hoffard?"

"Kerrect, Miss Wentworth."

"I've already told the *Bulletin* about my new business," Melissa said. "but word of mouth is better advertising, I am sure— so I'd thank you, Sheriff Ratchford."

"You're welcome, Miss Wentworth."

The sheriff left. He kept an eye open but Ric Williams didn't ride into town that day.

He checked Ric's office next morning at daybreak.

The door was still locked. He walked around to the back. That door also was locked.

Snorty wasn't in the barn.

He had a key to the front door. He had a key to every establishment in town, for that matter. He unlocked the front door and entered.

Ric's bed was made. He felt of the sheet.

It held no body heat. He checked things. Ric's saddle and riding gear were gone. So was his canteen and grubbag.

Fear entered him. Had Ric been ambushed—and killed—out on the range? He put Greg Mattson beyond suspicion. Greg was like his father, good old Scott Mattson—he fought openly.

Still, a man never knew . . .

But those three cowpuncher-farmers. . . . On Hell Crick. . . . Mebbeso Ric had tipped his hand the other day by telling them they were suspected of being cow-thieves?

Mebbeso they'd ambushed Ric, done away with him?

You're imaginin' things, Ike Ratchford. . . . This trouble had been piling up, piling up—it's got you on the raw edge, like it's got a lot of other people here. . . .

He saddled a buckskin and rode the ten miles south to the old Bar Diamond Bar spread. The world was growing green, he noticed—the rain had washed the dust from the cottonwoods and pines and they glistened in the rising sun.

Ric's old caretaker was feeding his chickens when the sheriff rode in. "Aim to talk a little to your boss," the lawman said.

"Ric isn't here, sher'ff."

The lawman scowled. "When last was he here?"

The old man considered this, hens clucking as they pecked grain. "Doggone me, sher'ff, I can't recollect to a day, but I think it was about a week ago—or along there."

"Close enough, an' thanks."

The lawman then cut across country heading northwest. The sun was acquiring heat rapidly. He rode at a walk or a long trot. He kept an eye on the horizon and when not watching the horizon he watched the earth, which was becoming powderdry.

He saw tracks of deer, elk, and cattle. Yes, and occasionally tracks of horses. This had been Bar Diamond Bar graze before Ric has sold all of his cattle.

Now Mattson Half Circle V stock grazed on his grass. When Bar Diamond Bar had sold out Half Circle V had doubled in acreage but wisely Greg Mattson had added no more head.

Thus each Half Circle V head had double its former grazing area. This showed in more beef per cow, Greg Mattson had once told the sheriff. The lawman figured Half Circle V ran over a range at least forty miles deep and the same distance in length.

Sheriff Ratchford had once figured out how many square miles Half Circle V stock grazed over. Forty times forty made sixteen hundred square miles. Each square mile held six hundred and forty acres. This Greg Mattson ran cattle on slightly over a million acres of Montana prairie.

And he paid not a cent in taxes or any other form for the use of the land. He paid his cowpunchers thirty dollars a month and found and a pair of good cowboy boots sold for fifty bucks and up.

The big cowmen had had their heyday, Sheriff Ratchford realized. Now they were through on government tax-free graze. Barbwire and windmills were moving in. These two would have to pay taxes. With taxes schools could be built, expenses paid, and the country would progress instead of stand still, as Black Butte town had done since built.

He hoped and prayed Greg Mattson would give in without causing gunsmoke and death. Ric had a good idea when he'd said that if Mattson caused trouble he'd see if soldiers couldn't be called in from Fort Assiniboine down southwest a hundred miles or so.

He searched for tracks left by a herd of cattle. He found none. The biggest bunch of tracks he saw he judged to be about ten head of cattle, no more.

And there had been tracks of cattle going down on Nameless Creek for water. He saw the cattle bedding down in the shade of timber along the creek. When rustlers stole they stole in big numbers. That was only common sense. And a big number made a lot of tracks.

He figured it about fourteen miles to the Sage Creek Meadow farmers. By that time his horse would have covered twenty-four miles, at the least. Finally Sage Creek was below him.

He drew rein and briefly rested his horse. Slouched in saddle, he gave himself over to the beauty of the land below, now green and growing from the recent long rain.

He found himself wondering if God had made such a beautiful land anywhere else in God's world. The meadows stretched out east and west with the creek—now down to normal flow—meandering this way, then that, as it lazily flowed to its junction with Black Butte River, six miles east.

He lifted his eyes to the land beyond Sage Creek. Hills rose, tumbled, became dim in the heated distance, then again rose from their mirage. And all the while high and black-crowned Black Butte to the northeast held its century-old silent guard of this mighty land.

Only then did he put the horse down the incline. When he came to the farm-settlement he found four of the new farmers out stringing wire around a homestead site.

The new farmers were now sober. The sheriff noticed each had a rifle close at hand, weapon usually leaning against the wagon or a nearby shrub. He asked if Ric had been out.

"Ain't seen him since the day you an' him visited," Jim Young said. "Should he have been here?"

The sheriff told them what he knew.

Jim Young said, "He's gone to Malty. He mentioned to me mebbeso he'd go there on some kind of business."

"That's undoubtedly where he went," the sheriff said. He went to turn his horse and Young grabbed the bridle-reins at the bit and said, "Sheriff, you ain't thinkin' nothin' bad's happened to Ric?"

"What could it be?"

"Ambush, mebbe?"

"Mattson is too big for that. Or, anyway, I think so."

"But thet damn' Kid Hannigan! He's

a killer! You can see it in his eyes, the way he packs that big pistol—how he kin shoot with it!"

Sheriff Ratchford had been thinking the same, something he hated to admit to himself.

"Or them other three farmers north of here on Hell Crick," Bob Winston said. "I ain't never met 'em but Jim says they look like hard-cases, all three of them."

"Don't draw verdicts on people you don't know," the sheriff said. "No, wherever Ric is, Ric's all right."

He realized he'd said that to give himself higher spirits. He debated about heading north and talking to the three cowpuncher-farmers. He did some mental arithmetic.

His buckskin had already carried him twenty-four miles. He figured some six miles, if not a mile or two more, to Hell Creek. From Hell Creek east to home would be another fourteen miles.

He totaled forty-four miles. Last night he'd read a Western story before sleep. The hero in this story had ridden the same horse about a hundred if not more miles within a few hours.

He smiled to himself, wishing he had such a horse. He crossed Sage Creek and rode toward the northern foothills a half-mile away. The long rain had really brought up the grass.

He figured mowers could cut the bluejoint inside of two weeks. Ric's Sage Creek farmers occupied some of the highest grass areas. That would not sit good with Greg Mattson.

For Mattson needed every spear of hay he could get for winter-feeding. Last winter he'd even run out of hay. His cattle had had to drift with blizzards to eventually die of hunger.

When he rode down on Hell Creek Jake Mullins came out of the brush, Winchester rifle in hand. "Didn't recognize you at first, sheriff," the soft speaking cowpuncher-farmer said.

"Got a guard out, eh?"

"Thought it best."

The sheriff looked ahead. George Hess was hoeing in his garden. Jake Mullins planted corn. Head crops were up and green.

Sheriff Ratchford asked if any of them had seen Ric. None had seen him since he'd delivered his warning.

"He missin'?" George Hess demanded.

"Anybody even think about doin' wrong to thet man an' he has me to deal with," Jake Mullins said.

"Repeat that fer me, too," Hess put in.

Griffin said, "Same goes for me."

"This ain't nothin' serious," the sheriff hurriedly said. "Don't go off half-cocked, boys. Ric might've jus' decided to ride south to do some business in Malta."

"Could be," Hess said.

Griffin said, "I'll ride into town tomorrow, sheriff. We need a bit of supplies, anyway, an' I'll check with you then."

Sheriff Ratchford nodded.

The buckskin was leg-tired when at last the sheriff rode into town. He racked the horse in his barn before a manger of hay and went to Ric's office. The office was still locked.

He unlocked the door. Wind rattled the windows despite the wood being swollen from the rain. Wind came in under the door, too.

The wind stirred papers on Ric's desk. For the first time, the sheriff picked one up and read it. It was addressed to him and dated two nights back.

He grimaced as he read. Then, he re-read. Then he said to the four walls, "I'm gettin' ol' an' I overlook points. Time was when I'd have looked for jus' such a piece of paper like this."

He put the note in his pocket.

"An I put myself an' Buck over forty miles of ridin'. Useless ridin', just because I didn't use my eyes."

He stood there—a bluff man, a blunt man, a hard man who could, when occasion demanded, be soft and yielding, a man who loved humanity and hated the evil and the evil doings of those he loved.

He said to the walls, "I wish there was some way a stupid ol' fool like me could kick himself in the ass."

The walls, of course, did not answer.

X

THIS WAS the morning of the day Sheriff Ike Ratchford made his long ride. Greg Mattson awakened at five that morning. He had a hell of headache. He'd sat alone in his office the night before killing a pint of Saddlemaker.

He'd sat with his boots on his desk and a pail of ice beside his swivel chair and a glass and the whiskey on the desk. He'd felt moody and all alone and he'd drunk automatically and, in a way, had enjoyed the misery his thoughts had plunged him into.

He hadn't even lit the Rochester kerosene lamp. He'd had the windows open to catch what little breeze there'd been for the summer night had been hot.

There were only two temperatures in Montana. Either boiling hot or freeze-cold, he'd thought.

He had a slough of money and property

but he wasn't happy. Maybe it was because he was unmarried and had no wife or get?

He then remembered boyhood friends who now were married and had families. They were unhappy, too—or so it seemed to him. He reached for the glass. It was empty, even the ice having melted.

He dropped his boots and picked the Bowie knife off the desk and hacked at the ice pail. The bucket was half-full of water for the ice had melted in the heat and the hunk of ice kept rolling away with each hack.

"Dammit," he told the ice. "You wanta stay in one piece, eh?"

He hacked faster and harder. Finally a chunk broke loose, but it was too big for his glass. He laid it on the desk. He hit it with the Bowie's handle. The ice skidded onto the floor.

He cursed hotly. "One of these days where everythin' goes wrong," he told the walls. "Now all I need is that damn' Hannigan's face to look at—an' the night would be completely ruined."

He tried to pick up the ice. It slithered from his grasp. He grabbed again; again, it escaped him. He fairly lunged forward. He got the ice under his forearm. He felt with his free hand.

He corraled the ice.

Just then a knock came to the door. It caught him on all fours. "Boss, you in?"

Damn it, anyway—Hannigan's voice.

"What'd you want?"

"That pinto horse—Patches."

"What's wrong with that piebald, pie-eyed bastardly geldin'?"

"He's down in his stall. Bloated big as a young elephant."

"Shoot the bastard?"

"Shoot him?"

"Yeah, shoot the—" Big Greg Mattson caught himself. I'm gettin' drunk, he silently told himself. This fool might take me word for word. "Where's he been grazin'?"

"Out on the south horse pasture."

"There's lupine grows there. He's et some of that. Get ol' Wad an' his long syringe and give the pinto the works from behind."

"Okay, boss. I'll report back."

"Not until mornin'. I'm tired. I'm goin' hit the hay soon."

"All right, boss."

Greg Mattson carried the ice corraled between his hands to his desk. He lay it with a book on each side. Then he hit with his Bowie's handle, the books imprisoning the ice. Finally it cracked into two pieces.

A smile broke across the grim face. He tried the smaller piece for size. It slid into the glass.

He poured whiskey over it. Then he put in a dash of ice-water. He over-filled the glass. Too much booze an' not enough water, he told himself.

Glass in hand, he settled back into his swivelchair. And at that moment, boots again stopped outside.

The young rancher tensed in his chair, fingers clutching the damp glass. That Hannigan—He was back again— This time he'd—

"Boss, you inside?"

Greg Mattson's muscles relaxed. The voice belonged to a cowpuncher he'd posted in town to watch Ric Williams' movements and also to see if any more farmers freighted themselves in.

"What is it, Lon?"

"Jus' rode in from town."

"More farmers?"

"No more farmers but Ric Williams is gone, boss."

"What'd you mean by gone?"

"He ain't in town. Wasn't in town all

day, to the best of my eyesight. Me, I think he was gone yesterday, too."

"You *think?* You don't *know?*"

"Not fer sure, boss. Sometimes he goes out the back door an' gets his hoss an' rides off through the brush an' a man lookin' from the front don't know whether he's gone or not."

"Then look from the back, damn it!"

"Man can't be two places at onct, boss."

"Where Ric go?"

"Nobody seems to know. The sher'ff —He was gone all day, too. I talked to him an' tried to fin' out where he was but I got a grunt or two outa him, no more."

"Ratchford always has been a talkative cuss." Greg Mattson said. "Mebbeso Williams is out at his ranch?"

"Not there. Loren an' Elmer are out there, keepin' an eye open. Loren sent Elmer into town to tell me the ranch has only the caretaker an' thet the sheriff was there early this mornin'."

Greg Mattson considered that. Plainly Sheriff Ratchford had gone to old Bar Diamond Bar to see if Ric Williams was there. That told him that the lawman apparently didn't know where Ric had gone, either.

"Ride back to town an' keep both eyes open, Lon."

"That I'll do, boss."

The boots left. Greg Mattson had lifted his glass again. He had scouts out watching both sets of farmers—those on Sage Creek, those on Hell Creek. He'd ride out and check with them come morning. He fell on his bunk completely dressed except for his boots and hat and immediately fell into a drunken, snoring sleep.

He automatically awakened at five, his usual rising-hour. He'd had but five hours of sleep, if that much—but he didn't feel sleepy. He shaved by sheer rote. He invariably kept himself close-shaven. He ate a big breakfast and then went to the horse pasture, two lumps of sugar in hand.

"Croppy, boy. Croppy, boy."

Croppy was a bay gelding, eight years old. He grazed with the other horses in the night-pasture. Greg Mattson noticed the grass had grown a lot in the last few days. That rain had been a lulu.

Croppy lifted his head. He had ears about an inch long—therefore the name Croppy, from crop-eared. He'd been a very early colt. A blizzard had come and the little fellow had frozen both ears down to nubs.

"Come on, you bay bastard— Sugar, Croppy. Sugar!"

Croppy came at a fast trot, tail up. Greg Mattson, ever the cowpuncher, noticed idly that bay's tail was rather long, and he made a secret memo to someday soon trim it shorter.

Mattson held the sugar in one hand and the other was hidden behind his back holding fifteen feet of light maguey rope, the loop already formed. Croppy was a wise one.

He'd come up for the sugar but have one eye roving around, and if you made the slightest movement toward him with your free hand—off he was on the dead gallop, escaping capture.

He wouldn't allow a man even to scratch his neck. For the man might suddenly grab him by the mane right behind the ears and then the man would have him prisoner.

And ahead would be a long and laborious and sweat-hot day under a heavy Navajo saddle-blanket with a heavy saddle over that and an even heavier burden—a rider— in the saddle.

As he nibbled sugar, his whiskey nose rubbing Mattson's palm, Mattson slowly drew in his hand, gently moving Croppy's head closer—and Croppy's roving eye roved even more, watching the left shoulder for if it moved the hand behind the back would suddenly appear—and he figured that hand held a noose.

The time came. Greg Mattson whipped the maguey noose free. Croppy immediately turned to bolt. The loop shot out. The maguey catch-rope was too short. The noose fell on Croppy's mane halfway down.

And Croppy, tail up, heels kicking, was gone.

Cursing under his breath, Greg Mattson pulled back the soap-weed rope. This day wasn't starting out too good, either. The coffee that damn' Chink cook had made for breakfast tasted as though it had been made with Bitter Creek's toughest alkali water. That Chink had cooked for old Scott—had come up from Texas with him, in fact—and he still couldn't make good Arbuckle.

Shorty Fillmore rode up on a blue roan gelding. "Open the gate an' I'll rope 'em for you, boss."

Mattson opened the wire gate. Shorty rode into the pasture. Mattson closed the gate. "Don't bust him, Shorty. I don't want him laid up."

"Soft an' easy, boss."

Shorty galloped toward the horses, catch-rope down. A few days before a cowpuncher had roped one of the ranch's top saddlehorses. He'd caught the horse on the dead run.

Instead of riding in close and taking up the slack in his rope the cowboy had put his roping-horse solidly and quickly on his rump, the slack immediately running out of the rope.

The cowpuncher had been tied hard-and-fast to his saddle's horn. The top horse had hit the end of the twine. He'd gone tail over head, landing hard on his back.

He didn't get up.

He'd broken his neck.

Mattson had been saddling a horse when this happened. He'd seen it clearly. He knew the horse was dead. He'd seen this busting before.

Mattson had started for the cowpuncher, rage in his heart, his face bleak.

The cowpuncher had read his boss's savage intentions. Fear had torn through him. There was just one thing to do—

Cut himself loose from the dead horse. His catch-rope was tied fast to the horn. He'd not have time to untie it. He whipped out his jackknife.

He slashed at the rope, cut it.

Then, low in saddle, he galloped away, bullets singing over him. And Greg Mattson had stood there, covered by dust, six-shooter yammering, not shooting to kill but just to scare.

"Thet son won't be back for his wages," the rancher had said. Then a sudden thought hit him. "Hell, thet horse he's on belongs to the ranch, don't it?"

"It sure does," his foreman had said. "But I got a hunch he'll leave the bronc in the livery down in town."

"He better, or he'll hang for a horsethief."

Now big Greg Mattson watched his cowpuncher lay the twine on Croppy. Croppy knew what was ahead. So did the rest of the saddle-horses in the pasture. They started out on the run away from the rider.

Croppy was smart. He ran in the center of the bunch, therefore he'd be harder to rope among the sea of heads. The cowpuncher missed two throws but snagged the crop-eared bay on the third.

The cowpuncher dallied. He brought Croppy to a slow halt, the other horse still running. He pulled Croppy in at halter-rope length and trotted back to Mattson, Croppy following.

"He's a smart little bastard, boss."

Greg Mattson almost said, "Wish some of the hands had the brains this bronc's got," but kept his mouth closed. "Thanks, friend." He rubbed Croppy's bony nose. "Come with me, you sly bastard."

Soon he had the horse saddled and ready. He stopped at the cook shack and the grumbling Chinese made him two sandwiches which he wrapped in an old sheet from an old Black Butte *Bulletin*.

First, Mattson rode to town, ten miles south along Black Butte River. The sheriff was home but nobody knew where the land-locator had gone. Mattson bought a pint of Old Rose at Kitty's, admired Melissa Wentworth's thin waist and beauty, wondered if he could make any time with the lady-gambler—and then decided he'd try that, after this trouble was settled.

He rode west along Sage Creek.

Croppy followed a wagon-road through the grass. The sight of the wagon tracks angered him.

A few months back, this road wasn't here. Farmers had made it. Ruts were cut deep. Already dust was gathering on their bottoms.

The tracks ran through Sage Creek's

best meadow-land. Here Half Circle V always cut its best hay. He found himself thinking of this land as his personal property.

It was not his. It belonged to Uncle Sam. Uncle had just let him use it free because nobody else had had any use for it. Now farmers were filing homestead-entries on this land.

They were putting the land to private use. They now owned the land. Greg Mattson's anger rose.

But with anger was logic. The *Stockman's Journal* last month had devoted its entire issue to the question of homesteaders moving in on a cow-outfit's graze.

It used as an example the cowman-nester trouble some years before down in Wyoming when Wyoming cattlemen had tried to gun-out homesteaders Nate Champion and his fellow sodbusters.

Cattlemen had killed Champion and his partner. They'd shipped in two trainloads of hired guns. These guns never were put to use. Public opinion and the law had stepped in first.

The cowmen had been defeated. The gunmen who'd gunned down Champion had been forced to flee for their lives ahead of the law, outlaws and fugitives. The homesteaders had won. They now lived in peace.

The *Journal* warned Montana cowmen. *Don't fight the homesteaders!* The cowmen would lose. Public opinion and the Law were against him. The cowman who had run an open range could now do but two things.

He could up-breed his stock. Buy purebred bulls and his cows would throw good calves. Longhorns had had their day. They were just bone and hide. Markets demanded good beef now.

Shorthorn, Angus, Herefords. . . . One good steer could tote three times the beef a longhorn carried. Better beef, too—marble-grained, tender. And one purebred ate no more—probably not as much—grass as a longhorn.

Thus the cowman could cut down on his range. He could grow more and better beef on one-third the range he'd used for longhorns. This cut down his expenses. Where he'd hired three men before he could now hire only one. Or maybe less. . . .

How would he get his land?

Through his cowpunchers? Almost all had homestead rights. Almost all swore never would they get callouses on their hands following a walking plow. They'd sport callouses where they sat down, yes— from a saddle, sir. But never from a pitchfork or a plow-handle.

Settle these cowpunchers on homesteads where there was tall grass and high water —the best spots on the range. Pay them while fulfilling homestead obligations to Uncle, and then transfer the property to your name.

A homestead didn't need much improvements. Uncle only called for a fence, a few acres plowed, a shack. And with a few years the cowpuncher would have a clear patent on his homestead. He'd own it, lock, stock, and barrel.

But all the time he'd been on the ranch's payroll. The ranch had paid him to homestead and the agreement was that for a few hundred more dollars he'd sign over his homestead to the ranch.

Cowpunchers never had much money. Two hundred bucks to one of them would probably be the biggest sum of money he'd ever have. Cowpunchers were fools. They worked for slave wages. They slept in bunkhouses that reeked of human stink and with dirty bedding crawling with bedbugs and other vermin.

Yes, this entire setup was changing. Yes, and changing fast. The cowpuncher's day was almost over. He would disappear with the longhorns. No more trail-drives of thousands of miles. No more riding for days and not opening a gate or seeing a fence.

Big roundups were over. Done with, finished. Now a man would call himself a cowpuncher as he rode along on an old plow-horse driving home the milk-cows. Or riding along a fence that was a few miles long seeing if the barbwire and posts needed repair.

Greg Mattson grinned. He'd made a big pretense of planning to run out these sodmen. But first, he'd try buying them. Hell, none of them had any money. Oh, a few dollars, no more—if they had any money—or brains—they'd not be trying to homestead.

For Greg Mattson knew this was marginal land—close to desert land. It lacked enough rain for successful farming. And what little rain came, came at any time of the summer.

He'd try these Sage Creek farmers out. See if they'd sell after proving-up, and Half Circle V paying them a few bucks a month for squatting, the agreement reading that after they'd got their final papers they'd sell to Half Circle V. Oh, for a hundred bucks, mebbso—no, he'd go to two hundred. But it would all have to be in writing.

The day of the verbal promise and the handshake was over. It had died with his father and with Brent Williams. Now all was paper, and signatures—and recordings, down at the county court-house. The day when a man's word was a man's bond was gone. Too many foreigners coming.

Nevertheless, wariness rode in the saddle with him. You could never tell about these newcomers. For all a man knew each and every one might be a wanted man in another state for everything ranging from molesting a woman to murder.

He neckreined Croppy across a quarter-mile of grass to ford Sage Creek and disappear in the hills.

Now Sagebrush Valley lay to his left as he threaded his way through scrub-pine and buckbrush. Soon the grouped wagons of the three farmers came into view in the southwest.

The wagons were bunched on Young's homestead. He remembered Young and Kid Hannigan close to blows during the last day of the Black Butte Stampede. Young had been pretty drunk and plainly he'd wanted trouble, bumping so deliberately into the Kid.

He dismounted with Croppy hidden. He took his field-glasses from their case and went ahead to squat in the protection of a bunch of big sandstone boulders.

He watched the farmers through the powerful glasses. They were cooking dinner. Young held a skillet over a small fire. He stirred the skillet's contents with a fork.

Greg Mattson scowled. Noontime, already? He glanced at the sun. Yep, chuck time.

He suddenly realized he was hungry. Breakfast was a long time and many miles back. He felt okay now that he'd been in the open air on a good horse. Nothing like open range and riding to clear away the booze-cobwebs.

He'd not eat with the farmers, though. Half Circle V had a linecamp two miles across Sage Creek Meadows at Dead Coyote Springs.

The linecamp had grub. He kept linecamps always stocked. When the Springs got low on water a cow might wade out in the blue ooze and bog down so he sometimes stationed a cowpuncher there.

He'd head for Dead Coyote and cook something.

But first, he'd parley with the damned farmers.

XI

Jim Young saw Mattson ride down-hill across Sage Creek. He handed the skillet to Smith Jones.

"Rider headed this way."

He put his field-glasses on Mattson. He adjusted the screw. "Damn things never the same. See good one time. Next time, way out of adjustment!"

The farmers watched Jones. Finally he lowered his glasses. "Greg Mattson."

Bob Winston reached for his rifle leaning on a wagon wheel.

"Don't get too ambitious," Young told the ex-policeman. "Unless he's got some weapons hid back of him on the hill, Mattson's alone."

Winston pulled back his hand.

Young again had the skillet. The big frying pan was heaping high with deer liver.

John Rogers had killed a five pronged buck this morning in the diamond willows along Sage Creek.

Young stirred the liver with a fork. "You know, sometimes I think I read too many of them damn' stupid Wild Bill Hickok an' Buffalo Bill stories when I was a young one."

"How come you say that?" Winston asked.

"Well, here I am, way out west—an' it ain't wild."

"I don't know for sure," Smith Jones said, "but here comes a man who claims we're squattin' on his lan'—an' he's got a rifle on his saddle an' a pistol on his hip."

When Mattson rode in he held his right hand high, palm out, in the redskin sign of peace.

The four exchanged wary greetings.

Mattson sniffed, "Deer liver?"

Young said, "Deer liver it is."

"Care for a bite?" Rogers asked.

Mattson shook his head. "Et jus' before I left town," he fabricated. He pulled a small smile to his lips. "You boys got some stakes out, I see—an' some bob-wire. You're squattin' on my best bluejoint hay land."

The four farmers didn't smile. Mattson noticed the one called Winston glanced at his rifle close at hand resting on its stock against a wagon-wheel.

171

Mattson said, "Think you'll homestead it to the finish?"

Again, he'd said the wrong thing. Actually, they might even think the sentence contained a threat, so he hurriedly said, "If you do get final papers—or drive that way—an' need a little money—"

He stopped. He was stumbling like a bronc in hobbles. Jim Young came to his assistance with, "I think I see yore point, Mr. Mattson. You might buy our homestead entries? Am I right on thet point?"

Mattson nodded. "We might work out something." Then he added, "Unless I kin run you off, first."

That was all bluff. Pure bluff. But it might work out. Have some effect. Behind him were some twenty odd cowpunchers. And the political power of huge and well-known Half Circle V.

And the gun of Kid Hannigan, too. Naturally word had got around how Kid Hannigan had outshot both himself and Ric Williams. Hell, these people thought he had hired Kid Hannigan as a gunslinger to turn against farmers.

Let them think that way. . . .

"Maybe we won't run?" Smith Jones' voice was hard.

Mattson shrugged. He saw no further use in talking to these men. His tongue had got him off on the wrong boot.

He looked at Jim Young. Grim face. He looked at Smith Jones and John Rogers and Bob Winston. And for a long moment hard and hot rage struggled inside the young rancher.

These damned eastern ex-cops were squatting on land he'd long considered belonging kit and parcel to Half Circle V. They were helping break to smithereens one of Montana's pioneer cow-outfits, carved out of this wilderness by the guns of his father and his father's cowpunchers against the Sioux, the Cheyenne, the Blackfoot—not to mention the deadly Crows.

Now that other men had died and bled and fought to build up this wilderness these bastards were coming in—and legally, too—to profit by the sweat and blood of men such as Brent Williams and Scott Mattson.

He held his temper, though.

He turned Croppy. "Take it easy, hands." He rode straight west toward the foothills. He was straightbacked. He knew that one of these could raise a rifle.

He could take aim. Let the hammer drop.

Drive a hard-nosed hunk of lead through his spine. They could bury him out here on this wilderness. And if the four kept their big mouths shut nobody would ever know what had become of him.

He thought of Ric Williams.

Nobody seemed to know where Ric was. Had somebody killed him and buried him out here on the range? He'd planned to ask the farmers if they'd seen Ric.

He hadn't had time.

He decided to scout the other farmers. They were the ones he suspected of cow-thievery. They'd been here since last fall. The four he'd just talked to had just arrived.

Later on they might steal his stock but not right now. They hadn't been here long enough. He then remembered the liver in the skillet. Maybe that wasn't deer liver?

Might be liver from a calf? A freshly-butchered calf, one of his spring calves?

This problem was getting complicated. It had a hell of a lot of tough angles. What would his father—Scott Mattson—have done in a similar situation? The answer to that, Mattson figured, was simple.

His father would have done the same that Ric Williams had done. Scott Mattson would have sold every head of longhorns he owned. He'd have homesteaded for himself —if he'd not already homesteaded Half Circle V's buildings—and hired cowpunchers to homestead.

He'd go beyond Ric Williams. He'd have bought pureblooded cattle—Angus, Shorthorn, Herefords—and started over again. And undoubtedly within a short time he'd be producing as much—if not more—tonnage in beef on a hell of a lot less steers and with a much greater profit.

Mattson fried eggs and bacon after baking biscuits in the linecamp. His mother had always kept a bunch of hens on hand. He still had many hens, thus the eggs, delivered last Friday by the ranch hostler.

Half Circle V was one of the few ranches in Montana that had fresh milk and not milk out of the can. His mother had seen to it that the ranch always had a milk-producing cow or two.

The day was blistering hot. Croppy chewed bluejoint in the lean-to barn in the shade.

Greg Mattson dozed off for an hour. A terrible dream awakened him. He sat up and looked about and then remembered where he was. He held his head in his hands.

He was sweating but not from the nightmare. Nightmare sweat is cold. This sweat was hot.

Outside the sun hit with such heat you'd swear it was trying to pick up every drop of rain that had fallen during the rain-spell.

Nevertheless, a man and horse had to move through it.

He searched for cow-tracks. He found some but not those of a herd of any size. As he rode north, the tracks fell back. Almost every head he missed had been runoff his northern range.

North was Canada and Indian reservation. He'd ridden north as far as Timber Mountain, Saskatchewan. Timber Mountain had had a mild gold rush. He'd figured his beef had gone there to feed itinerant gold-seekers.

He'd discovered different. Royal Canadian Mounted Police had the situation there well under control, as usual. No Half Circle V beef was being smuggled into Canada.

Timber Mountain miners ate Canadian beef and Canadian beef only, the Mounties said. They'd doubled their guard along the Montana-Saskatchewan border.

And well he knew you couldn't bribe a Mountie.

He'd also checked at Indian Reservations. There was at that time a political struggle between the Army and the Department of Interior for control of the Indians and their reservations.

For the Indian was a healthy plum. Forced onto reservations, it took millions of dollars to feed and clothe and house him and his during the year—and the two government departments each sought control for the money involved.

Reservation agents were caught in the middle. Their well-paid jobs were at stake, not to mention side-graft in purchasing supplies for the redskins. Thus for some time—until their fate was decided—they were forced to play the game honestly.

No bribes, no side-money from dishonest sutlers, nothing out of ordinary—who wanted to lose a very high-paying job for a few bucks coming in from stolen cattle?

After this question of management was settled, yes—definitely yes, but until then, play it cool and honest, friend.

But cows couldn't fly. Cows left tracks behind. This was a riddle. Most cattle had disappeared from the north end of his huge range. And yet there was no market for them up north.

Miles and miles of worthless badlands lay to the west. Without water and with only occasional salt grass, they were uninhabitable, their only occupants a few bobcats, some coyotes and the animal both the cats and coyotes lived off of—the lowly cottontail rabbit.

No cows would wander into that worthless area. If so, hunger and thirst would drive them east onto water and grass again.

East lay Hungerford's Pitchfork outfit that ran all the way east to the Dakota line. And the wealthy Hungerford family surely wasn't stealing cattle. That eliminated Pitchfork.

And the Hungerfords made sure no stolen cattle crossed their graze. Rustlers had tried before and had been gunned down.

The cattle had to be going south.

He'd checked with Sheriff Ratchford. Ratchford had then checked along the Great Northern rails where the new population—the farmers—were settling rapidly.

He'd checked as far as west as Pacific Junction and as far east as the Dakota line. He'd come back with the report that the state's Stockman's Association had detectives out watching the area for stolen beef. Every beef delivered to a butcher shop there had to be stamped and passed by the Association. And the Association did not tolerate thieves, Greg Mattson well knew.

Dusk was heavy when he halted a tired horse on the south rim of Hell Creek valley, the shacks of the three farmers below him— the farmers that had been cowpunchers and now hung onto the handles of a walking-plow.

It was time to light the old Rochester kerosene lamp but none of the *jacals* had lights, he quickly noticed. Evidently none of the farmers was home? Or maybe they sat in the gathering dark without lights for lamps attracted mosquitoes?

Mosquitoes were a terror here on this northern range. Only the howling of the wind made any kind of living permissible during mosquito season, which lasted from spring to winter.

Here the wind stopped blowing only two times a day—at dawn and at sunset. Without a strong wind, mosquitoes swarmed in by the millions. Range horses took it on the run.

They gathered in groves of cottonwoods or boxelders. Mosquitoes will not stay in an area smelling of manure. Thus when the horses entered their groves the manure smell drove the mosquitoes away.

Mosquitoes do not bother cattle like they do horses. Thus cows fared better but still got well-bitten.

When night came, the mosquitoes departed. Sitting there slouch-saddle on the rimrock, big Greg Mattson waited for lights to come into life in the cabins below—but none came.

Finally he decided the cabins were without occupants. Nevertheless, wariness was in him. He came in from behind hidden by the creek's trees. He left his horse and went ahead on foot, rifle in hand.

For the thought had come that perhaps these three were out stealing cattle. He approached the house of George Hess. A dog came out barking but, as he barked, he wagged his tail. It was still light enough to notice this and Greg Mattson hunkered and quietly said, "Come on, mutt, come on."

He had a small piece of jerky beef he'd had in his saddle-bag. The dog came closer, sniffing. He'd stopped barking but the two dogs at the two other cabins had taken up a raucous yapping.

The dog gulped the meat. He moved in and Greg Mattson played with the dog's long ears. The dog liked that. He sat down next to Mattson, who paid his attention to the cabins.

Had any cabin been occupied surely the dogs would have brought that occupant out into the open to investigate, but no doors opened. Soon the Half Circle V owner was behind Hess' cabin.

Hess' barn was empty.

Greg Mattson then went to the other two barns. Neither held a horse but both held a couple of cows. He knew what property—real or moving—that each homesteader had. He'd made that his business early. You had to know what your enemy had in line of fire and mobility, you know.

Each had but one saddle horse. Each had four head of work horses. Greg Mattson looked out into their pastures. By lying flat on the ground bellydown he saw clearer in the uncertain light.

The work horses were on pasture. He could see their legs. He then squatted and idly rubbed a collie behind the ears. Where were these cowpunchers who had turned hoeman?

Out rustling his cattle, maybe? Anger and rebellion struck the big young rancher. His jaw hardened. He felt powerless. The night made him a prisoner. Were it daylight possibly he could have traced the three and determined which way they had ridden, at least.

There was nothing he could do here. He went openly to his horse and mounted, one dog following him. He pointed Croppy southeast toward Black Butte town.

His ranch was directly east. It was closer than the cowtown but he wanted a drink in Kitty's and a hot meal at the Longhorn. He was halfway to town when he heard hoofs ahead coming toward him.

He pulled off into a coulee, dog following. The night now was dark. He could not see the riders. They were heading toward Hell Creek. One sang in a voice soaked by booze.

Greg Mattson cocked his head, trying to place the voice. He did not recognize it. Suddenly the dog darted away, heading for the riders, some hundred yards south.

The booze-singing stopped. The hoofs stopped. Mattson heard a man say, "By God, that's my dog Shep! Now what the hell is he doin' out here this far from my cabin?"

"Must've been headin' for town lookin' for you, Hess."

Mattson then knew the horsemen were

the three farmers heading for their homesteads. Evidently they'd merely ridden into town. His theory of their being on his range rustling his cattle evaporated. This definitely hadn't been a good day.

"Come on home, you ol' sonofabitchin' dog," Hess said and then added, "We're ridin' like our broncs are wind-busted. Let's put a few miles ahin' us in a hurry, eh?"

"Suits me."

The horses broke into a hard lope. Soon their hoofsounds had run out against distance and once again Greg Mattson took the wagon trail leading to the town his father and Brent Williams had laid out and built.

Black Butte town held but a few lights when the Half Circle V owner rode in, Croppy feeling the many miles he'd put behind him since sunup. The Longhorn was closed but a few lights showed in the saloon and he swung down there and twisted reins and stalked inside, chap-wings swishing, bootheels pounding, long-shanked star-rowelled spurs clanging.

Three men were at the bar. Nobody was at the tables. He wished Melissa Wentworth had been at a table. He would have liked to see her loveliness again.

One of the men at the bar was Sheriff Ike

Ratchford and the other two were Malcolm Stewart and a man Mattson did not know.

The sheriff introduced the stranger. "Mr. Clarence Maresh, Uncle Sam's top land agent, comin' up from Malta. Clarence, Mr. Greg Mattson, owner of Half Circle V."

A stiffness entered Malcolm Stewart. Mattson and Maresh shook hands, Mattson knowing full well that this well-dressed tall man knew he and his ranch were against the farmers on his range—and those yet to come.

Kitty broke the tension by coming downstairs at that moment, long dressing gown making her square shape even more unfeminine.

"Heard your voice from upstairs," she told Mattson. "Are you hungry, Greg?"

Mattson smiled. It was good to have somebody thinking of you. "I could eat the—" He stopped, grinned. "Anythin' you cook, Kitty."

"Your mount?"

"Croppy."

Kitty spoke to the bartender. "I'll take over here, Jake. See that Croppy's stabled, has oats and plenty of hay."

The bartender went out back. Kitty O'Neill moved her bulk into the kitchen.

Greg Mattson reached over the bar and

snagged a bottle of Musselshell Beer from the ice box. He opened it with his jackknife and drank, the cold brew sweet against his dust-filled throat.

Sheriff Ratchford said, "Well, my nightcap is down, so I'll head for home, gentlemen. You comin' with me, Malcolm?"

"For my bed, too," the ex-schoolteacher said.

Clarence Maresh said, "And this man for his bed upstairs. I'm sorry I didn't get to see Mr. Williams. I hope he's in his office tomorrow."

Mattson spoke to the sheriff. "Ric ain't in town?"

"Hasn't been for some days."

Mattson scowled. "Where do you suppose he is?"

"I don't know. He said nothin' to me about leaving. Mr. Maresh came up from Malta to see him."

"Think somethin' happened to him?" Mattson asked.

Malcolm Stewart listened. Clarence Maresh listened.

"I don't know," the sheriff said. "I've looked around an' found nothing. Well, goodnight, folks."

The sheriff and Stewart left. Maresh said,

"Glad to have met you, Mr. Mattson," and Greg Mattson returned the salutation. Maresh started climbing the stairs.

Mattson watched the man leave. Kitty rattled a pot in the kitchen. Mattson smell ham and hoped she'd add about half a dozen eggs to it, and a few gallons of hot coffee.

His mind went to Ric Williams. Where in the hell had Ric gone? A touch of fear hit him. Had Ric discovered who'd been stealing Half Circle V cows? And had he died under gunfire?

He then thought, none of my damn' business. . . .

Or was it?

XII

Ric Williams knew there would be no peace on Black Butte range until this cow-stealing business was stopped—if indeed there'd be peace then. He knew he could never settle farmers on Black Butte grass as long as the farmers were suspected of rustling.

He was sure his first group of farmers on Hell Creek were not cow-thieves. He'd watched these three all winter and was pretty sure they were not riding out nights to steal Greg Mattson's Half Circle V stock.

Still, a man could not be sure. . . . Anyway, this rustling would have to be stopped.

He'd made one error, though—he later discovered. He should have told Sheriff Ratchford that he was leaving and would try to solve this stealing. But he'd not done this, so that was that.

Within a few days he'd covered the northern route of investigation that Greg Mattson had earlier covered. He discovered the same facts that his long time school-opponent had learned.

No stolen cattle went into Canada. The Indian reservations were using none, either. None was being driven across Pitchford range to the east. There were but two directions the stolen cattle could go.

One was west, into the naked, ugly badlands. They could not be held there without hay being hauled in and water also being delivered. The other direction was south.

The end of the fifth day he sat in a saloon in Malta and used his eyes and ears. He'd picked out one of the lowest dives in the skidrow section along Milk River in the cottonwoods and mosquitoes.

He was unshaven and his clothes were dirty but he'd bathed in Milk River before riding into this redlight district. He soon discovered something new to him. Miles south in the Little Rocky Mountains there was a gold boom.

Placer gold had recently been discovered. Two gold-towns had sprung up over night. He'd heard that a least ten thousand miners and families and mine-owners were congregated in the two towns.

Gold had been discovered late last fall.

Greg Mattson had started losing cattle about that time, Ric remembered. The thousand mouths needed a lot of meat.

Two hours later, he was riding south. He figured it about sixty miles from Malta to the first gold-town. The country consisted of rolling land. Two big cow-outfits ran cattle in this region.

They were the Turkey Track and the Mill Iron. Both were tough, hard-boiled Texas outfits who'd driven thousands of worthless longhorns up the Montana Trail some twenty years back.

Both outfits had a tough record in regard to cow-thieves. Each hanged a man even if only suspected of rustling. Thus cow-thieves stayed away from Turkey Track and Mill Irons brands.

Ric felt sure neither Turkey Track or Mill Iron lost beef to rustlers. For one thing, a rustler usually never stole from an outfit close at hand. To do so would bring suspicion down on him . . . and the hangman's noose. Thus he stole from distant outfits.

Ric spent three days in the first mining town and two in the second. Both were mad, gold-crazy towns with many saloons, whorehouses and no schools or churches. And both had many mouths to feed.

He made the rounds of the mine commissaries and butcher shops posing as a rancher with beef to sell. His ranch, he said, was south across the Missouri in the Musselshell basin. He sold not an ounce of beef.

Each commissary and butcher-shop bought beef from an outside source, he learned—but he was not told where that source originated. This he had to discover on his own hook.

He'd never been in the little Rocky Mountains before. Once when a child he and his father had had a reason to ride to the Mill Iron. He'd then seen the mountains in the southwest distance.

He'd never forgotten them. His father had told him that they were the last extension of the Big Rocky Moutains in Montana. Brent Williams had said that the last chain was the Black Hills of Dakota.

His father had known a lot about geography.

He was sure nobody he knew was in this area. Word of the gold rush might have reached secluded Black Butte town but if so he couldn't remember hearing about it.

While in the nearest town, he saw but one man he knew—and why this man was in the gold-crazy town, he then did not understand.

He'd decided to secretly watch the biggest commissary in town. Sooner or later, somebody would deliver beef to it. He'd then trail this somebody and see, if possible, where the beef came from, for he was sure the entire area lived on stolen beef—beef bought cheaply from the cow-thieves.

He made camp on the mountain beside the commissary. Night and day, the town and its stampmills clanged and screeched and hollered. Others camped on the hills—miners looking for work, women, children.

The second day of watching he saw a man below talking to the butcher and head-cook of the commissary. The three stood in the alley. Ric put his field-glasses on the newcomer.

He watched, heart beating strongly. His glasses clearly showed the man. Finally the man walked away. He fell out of sight. Ric Williams lowered his glasses, still doubting his eyes.

For the man had been chunky, wore range-clothing, and a black beard covered his square face. The man was none other than Kid Hannigan.

What was Kid Hannigan doing here? Had Greg Mattson canned him and had the gunman come here looking for work?

Or did he work with the cattle-thieves? Was he here to sell stolen Half Circle V beef?

Ric never saw Kid Hannigan again but that evening four wagons drove in behind the commissary, their loads covered by dirty tarpaulins. Each wagon had a double-box which meant they each carried quite a load.

Ric was squatting under a pine tree playing a listless game of whist with a miner offshift. "What's that?"

"What's what?"

"These wagons. Behind the commissary."

The miner looked. "Them's beef wagons. They come in about every three, four days. Deliverin' beef to the commissary."

"Wonder where they come from?"

"Damn' if'n I'd know. Your play, friend."

Ric laid down his cards. "Jus' remembered I got to meet the boss of the Circle Bar. He promised to meet me at this time. Yesterday. Said he might have a table open for me."

Ric posed as an itinerant gambler.

Within a few minutes, he was behind the commissary, hidden in a shed, watching the wagons being unloaded not more than forty feet away.

He learned nothing about the beef. The meant packed no hides, therefore no brands. The beef had been dressed out and cut into quarters. But he did later learn who had hauled in the meat.

"Them beef haulers," a man said. "Them's the Cullen gang, mister. Tough bunch. Got a camp down below on the mountain. Clyde Cullen jus' a week or so kilt Tike Qualey?"

"I'm new here," Ric said. "Tike Qualey?"

"Was our town marshal," the gambler said. "Tough bastard from Texas. Town-tamer then, I heard. Fast gun, but Clyde Cullen was faster."

"What'd they fight about?"

"Damn' if I know. Cards or no cards?"

Later Ric heard that the marshal had accused Clyde Cullen of rustling beef because how in the hell could a man raise so much beef on a mere quarter section of land with only one old milk cow in evidence?

Ric also learned about the Cullen farm,

two miles south of town on the level country.

A farmer had owned the homestead. One day he'd mysteriously disappeared. The Cullen clan had then moved in.

Nobody knew where the farmer had gone—that is, if he had departed. . . .

Ric camped in the pines from which he overlooked the Cullen farm. He did not have to wait long.

Three days later seven wagons left the farm, heading north. Each spring wagon-seat held a driver. Ric had seen the drivers around town—mostly bearded, tough-looking men.

Each had packed a pistol on his hip. All had the looks of cow-punchers, not mule-skinners or farmers. Swaggering men, who usually traveled in two or threes. . . .

Each wagon sported a very high box. That meant each could carry double the ordinary load. Each wagon was pulled by four horses abreast.

The three Cullens rode ahead. Each led an unsaddled horse. That horse told Ric they'd ride hard and fast to wherever they were going, changing from one horse to the other.

Ric followed, hiding in the pine and

spruce footing the Little Rocky foothills. Twenty miles north he ran out of such protection. He then followed coulees and draws far to the west of the wagons.

The three Cullen brothers had long ago ridden out of sight in the blue haze of distance. Ric had seen them close in the mining town. He had judged them to be in their twenties.

Each packed a great family resemblance. Ric figured that until you got to know each well only then could you tell Clyde from Ed and Ed from Lon and Lon from Clyde.

All were short, stocky men. All wore old range-garb—runover boots, clanging spurs, blue jeans, faded shirts—and each packed a gun on his hip, and two, he'd noticed, had their guns tied down.

Plainly the three expected trouble . . . and were prepared for it. They hung together; where one was, his two brothers were.

Ric figured the man who was foolish enough to challenge one had the other two on his hands, whether he liked it or not.

He also noticed all wagons carried a load, tarps covering this. He wondered what the loads consisted of.

The wagons followed the Malta road until

they reached the northern end of the mountains. Here they departed from that road and continued on northwest on what appeared to be a new road.

Ric's glasses showed it held deep ruts. That told him wagons had gone over it during the last rainspell.

If the wagons continued in this direction they'd cross the Milk some twenty miles west of Malta, Ric figured. They'd then head into the rough badlands constituting Half Circle V's western border.

Things were beginning to add up, Ric figured. These thieves apparently drove stolen cattle west into the badlands. This could be easily accomplished. They were smart bastards.

Ric deduced that the three Cullen brothers had ridden ahead to shove Mattson steers into the badlands, an easy task.

Cattle grazed to the edge of the rough country. All a rider had to do was circle a few head and haze them into the badlands. Other riders could pick them up, chase them west, and soon the badlands would have them completely hidden.

Ric moved from one point to another. Almost every hill was crowned either with big sandstone and granite boulders or scrub pine and stunted cottonwoods or boxelders.

He moved at night. After the wagons made night-circle he'd come down in the dark and ride ahead twenty miles or so, finally picking out the spot where undoubtedly the wagons would reach the next day.

This was easy to determine. Wagons leave tracks. Points where men camp are sure to have debris left behind to mark their locations.

Ric then picked out a high butte to hide on. He'd bought grub in the Little Rocky Mountains and he supplemented this by cottontail rabbits he caught with horse-hair snares he'd made from the mane or tail of his horse.

Three nights later, the wagons came to the Milk River. They were further west of Malta than he'd reckoned. If they continued on this angle they'd be in the badlands about thirty miles west of Black Butte town —and in a region only a few outlaws would pass through, for no cowpuncher had reason to ride in this waterless, grass-free area.

He kept close watch of the land below and of this back-trail. For hours he squatted looking southeast toward the mountains, now hidden by distance, but he discovered no riders.

The cow-thieves had picked their trail well for each night's stop was close to a spring or a small creek heading north, a tributary of the Milk River.

That night the wagons made camp in Milk River's cottonwoods. Ric was surprised next morning to see two big water-wagons move north with the others. These water-wagons had evidently been stationed along the river awaiting the other wagons.

He still did not know what was under the tarpaulins. The wagons began moving northwest toward a canyon leading out of the badlands some few miles away.

Ric rode down-river into Malta. His father had been a friend of the Malta sheriff who had once sheriffed the Black Butte area until his father and Scott Mattson had split the country to make Black Butte town a county-seat and Sheriff Ike Ratchford its lawman.

"You're Richard Williams, ain't you?" the sheriff asked.

"The same, sheriff. Why ask?"

"Brent Williams' boy?"

"I am."

Ric knew the sheriff hadn't seen him for

years. He learned that Sheriff Ratchford had a bulletin out for him.

"Seems like you suddenly disappeared, Mr. Williams, an' Ike Ratchford's worried about you."

Ric said, "I'll square things with him." He then told the sheriff about the wagons and the Cullen brothers. "Where'd the wagons cross the Milk?" the lawman asked.

Ric told him. "Squaw Crossing."

"That's west of my line of jurisdiction, Mr. Williams. My line is two miles east of Squaw Crossin' at Willow Point. That's in Sheriff Ratchford's territory." His seamed eyes narrowed. "This is a kinda wil' tale, young man."

"I know that, but it's true."

"So far them wagons ain't done nothin' unlawful. You got no concrete evidence they're out to haul back stolen beef."

"You ever hear of the Cullen brothers?"

"Sure have. I'll tell you about 'em."

The Cullens were Canadians. They were wanted up north for train and bank robberies. They'd fled into the United States about five years before, the Malta sheriff related.

"Some claim they work with the Cassidy bunch now an' then, holdin' up banks, but nobody can prove that. Far as I know, there are no charges against any of the three in Montana."

"Why don't the law take them into custody and notify the Mounties?"

The sheriff grinned. "I don't work for the Royal Canadian Mounted Police," he pointed out. "Good day, Mr. Williams."

Ric went downtown. By sheer accident he met young Sam Hoffard coming out of Koke Saddlery.

"All the country's lookin' for you, Mr. Williams. Some even claim somebody's shot you down on open range an' killed you."

Ric noticed a wagon and team tied to the Saddlery hitching-rack. The wagon contained two upright stitching machines.

"You driving out to Black Butte?" Ric said.

"I sure am. Leavin' right now. Them's the sewin' machines for Miss Melissa's new business there. I'm drivin' 'em out to her. Goin' drive all night. Cooler then an' easier on my horses an' a man an' team makes better time."

"Can you wait a minute or two?"

"Sure can. Why?"

"I'm going to bum some paper and a pencil somewhere. I want you to take a letter out to Sheriff Ratchford.

"Deliver it to him first thing on reachin' Black Butte.

Mr. Koke inside will have paper and pencil for you, I'm sure."

Ric wrote rapidly but to the point. He then addressed the envelope and sealed it. Hoffard put the envelope in his shirt's breast-pocket and buttoned his vest over it.

"Sure can't lose it now," he said.

"You deliver that in the morning, and I'll buy the first saddle you make in Black Butte, and I give my word on that."

"Your word's good with me, Mr Williams."

XIII

SHERIFF IKE RATCHFORD was frying his ham and eggs the next dawn when he saw young Sam Hoffard unlatching the front gate. "Now what the hell is wrong?" the sheriff asked himself.

He was in a surly, unhappy mood. He'd been searching the range for any signs of young Richard Williams. He'd climbed buttes and scouted with his field glasses and he'd seen riders crossing this wilderness but always they turned out to be one of three classifications.

The first group were drifters. With spring-roundup finished ranches laid off riders until fall beef-gather was started some months away. Thus there was a surplus of jobless cowpokes riding here and there either riding the grubline or looking for riding jobs which weren't.

The second group was the seven head of farmers Ric had moved in. The third and most abundant group were Greg Mattson's

Half Circle V riders going about various range chores.

He even found himself wishing that Montana had buzzards. Were there buzzards a man could tell where every dead thing lay on this wide range—be this cow or horse or man or what have you.

You could see buzzards circling in the sky and ride that direction, but here there were no winged carnivores except magpies, and these only cleaned up on winter-killed cows. He'd never heard of a magpie—that gaudy and saucy black and white bird—that had ever stuck his bill into a dead human.

He went to the door, spatula in hand. "You're the young man who's gonna work for Miss Melissa in her saddle-shop, ain't you?"

"I am. I got a letter for you."

"Letter? When'd you start workin' for the postal service?"

Sam Hoffard smiled. This sheriff was a crusty old character, no two ways about that. "Mr. Williams gave it to me to give to you last evenin' when I left Malta."

"You mean—Ric Williams?"

"Yeah, the land agent."

"You saw him in Malta? Last night? How

is he? In good shape? He's been gone—hell, lotsa days."

"He tol' me this letter'll explain all that."

Sheriff Ratchford elatedly dug in his pocket. "Ric pay you? If he didn't I will an'—"

Hoffard backed away. "Ric offered to pay me but I said no dice. He then tol' me he'd buy the first saddle made—that I made, too—in Black Butte."

"I'll buy your first bridle. Headstall, reins and bit—not an ear-split headstall, but one that buckles under the jaw! An' a plain curb bit, not a spade-bit—one them chokers! Not one of them by any means!"

"I thank you, sir."

Young Sam Hoffard left. Sheriff Ratchford got a butcher knife and slit open the envelope. First he read rapidly, then he read the second time more slowly, and the third time he read very, very slowly, lips moving.

The letter digested, he stood and stared out the window at his garden, seeing not his carefully hoed spuds and radish and turnips—his mind darting here, then there.

Should he call in Greg Mattson on this? He debated this but for a moment. Naturally Mattson would be called in. They were stealing Mattson's cattle, weren't they?

And Mattson had a crew of tough cow-punchers. Men like that Kid Hannigan —Suddenly the sheriff's eyes pulled narrow. Hell, he'd not seen Hannigan for some days—about as many days as Ric Williams had been gone.

Greg Mattsn didn't know where Hannigan had gone, either.

But now he knew where that gun-throwing bearded bastard had gone. Ric's letter had told him.

Three days ago Greg Mattson had been in town and asking if anybody had seen Kid Hannigan.

"How come you hire a gunman?" Sheriff Ratchford had asked.

"Gunman?" Greg Mattson's gray eyes had stabbed holes through the lawman. "Who t'hell said Hannigan was a hired gun?"

The sheriff had shrugged. "Everbody aroun' here. Hell, he's liquid fire with his cutter, Greg. He showed thet when he outshot both you an' Ric Williams when the stampede was on a few weeks ago."

"Jus' 'cause a man's good with a weapon is no sign he's a gunman," the young Half Circle V owner said shortly. "I hired him to punch cows, not sling a gun."

Sheriff Ratchford wisely had kept silent.

"I ain't ready to sling guns with Ric Williams an' his farmers," Greg Mattson continued. "From what I've heard, Ric's done sent orders down to Malta to send in no more farmers. For all I know, he might have given up his big idea of becomin' a gentleman land-locater." He laughed cynically. "Gentleman did I say? Ric Williams a gentleman? I must be slippin' my picket pin in this heat—"

"Some one of these days one of you'll kill t'other," the sheriff said. "An' all because of nothin'."

"Nothin', you say?" Greg Mattson had sobered. "You said it, sheriff! Over nothin', absolutely nothin', damn it to hell!"

"Then how come you hired Hannigan?"

"Because he came recommended to me as an all aroun' cow-hand, which he sure as hell is."

"Mind if I ask who recommended him?"

"Not a bit. Frien' of mine. Big wheel for the Stockman's Association down in Helena."

"How come he recommended Hannigan?"

"God damn, sheriff, but you're full of questions today. Here I'd just asked if you'd seen Kid Hannigan an' you want a life history of him from me. Friend said Hannigan was his brother-in-law an' Hannigan needed a job an' I said send him on and he was sent on. Thet answer your questions?"

"Don't get rough with me, Greg!"

Greg Mattson had studied the old sheriff. "If it was my day to laugh, I'd sure as hell laugh, Ratchford. But I laugh only on Fridays an' this is Wednesday."

Breakfast finished, Ratchford went to his barn, led his sorrel gelding out and pumped a bucket of water for the horse, then saddled and bridled and swung up.

He looked down at his empty rifle-scabbard. Then he dismounted and went to the house and returned carrying his Winchester .30–.30. He put the rifle in the boot and led the horse to the gate and once outside swung up and rode north toward Half Circle V.

He rode at a running-walk, shod hoofs kicking up little whirls of dust. The effects of the long rain were almost gone. Already grass was turning brown. He looked at the western sky. Far off on the horizon were a few dark clouds. Rain here invariably came from the west or northwest.

It was rain from the Pacific coast that hadn't fallen on the Pacific Range or the

Rocky Mountains. Very seldom did rain here come from the east or from the south.

Greg Mattson was breaking a blue roan gelding to saddle, for he rode the ranch's rough-string. He claimed that you had to teach a horse how to buck. He said a bronc bucked because he'd been trained to buck or because he was afraid.

And once a horse got into the bad habit of bucking he wanted to buck every time a man swung up on him. Sheriff Ratchford agreed with this. He'd broken every head of his personal saddle-horses himself. Although stove-up and not young, he still broke broncs.

But not a one had a chance to buck. He first tied one in a stall. He fed him hay and oats. He made friends with the horse. Then he saddled and unsaddled, getting the bronc used to the saddleblanket and saddle and hackamore.

Finally he swung gently into leather, time after time, the horse tied to the stall. Thus he got the horse used to his weight. Finally, after a month or so of this, he got the horse in the open, and gently eased into saddle.

If the bronc threatened to buck, the sheriff pulled his head up with the hackamore's rope—for long ago he'd learned a horse cannot buck if he can't get his head down between his legs.

He turned the bronc in a circle, this way, then that, until all desire to pitch had left the green horse. He didn't ride far that first week. Just a few miles a day, no more.

He rode with a hackamore pipe for about a month before he used a bridle and bit, and then the bit was a plain snaffle, nothing more, for he didn't want to bit-gall the bronc's tender mouth.

And in a short time, he had a horse—a real tough cow-horse, one that knew him and one he knew. This was the way Greg Mattson broke Half Circle V's rough-string, also.

Greg Mattson saw the sheriff riding in and he turned from the road toward the breaking-pasture gate. He awaited Sheriff Ratchford's arrival and as the sheriff pulled in the rancher said, "I ain't as bitin' as the other day in town. This time I'm worse."

"You need a spring dose of sulphur an' molasses." the sheriff said. "I mind your good momma givin' you such each spring."

Mattson smiled, "You remember right, sheriff. Anybody seen hide or hair of that damned fool of a Ric Williams?"

"I got a letter from him today."

"Letter?" Mattson scowled. "The idiot done got so scared of me he done fled the country?"

"Here it is, Greg."

While Mattson read, the roan stood hip-humped, acting like an old broke saddler. Sheriff Ike Ratchford admired the four-year-old. He'd soon be able to run a wide circle and run the wild ones out of the badland brakes.

Mattson handed back the letter. "Don't concern me in the least," he said.

The sheriff studied him. "He's trackin' down whoever mebbeso is stealin' your Half Circle V cattle."

He emphasized the word *your*.

"I never asked him to," Mattson pointed out.

Sheriff Ike Ratchford kept a straight face but inside he was surprised and mystified. He'd expected this tough man to want to immediately saddle and ride out for the cowthieves.

"You're losin' money," the sheriff said.

"I got a lot of money. Too damn' much, in fact. There are three danged beautiful women down in town. Martha, Jennie an' Miss Wentworth. An' you know what?"

"What?"

"My money's made me so damn' suspicious of thinkin' a woman would marry me only because she wanted my money thet my life is becomin' cramped aroun' any of them three, an' it hurts me. I mean that."

Now it was Sheriff Ratchford's turn to be cynical. "My heart bleeds for you," he said. "You ever hear of the Cullen gang?"

"I have. An' I have no desire to tangle guns with 'em. I'm a young man an' I look forward to a middle age of work and an old age of jus' sittin' an' rememberin'."

"He saw Kid Hannigan in the Little Rocky Mountains."

"So the letter says. I reckon the Kid went there to try to get some of thet gold, which of course he won't get."

"Mebbeso Hannigan's workin' in cahoots with the Cullens, stealin' stock he was hired to pertect?"

"That happened afore, I've heard an' read."

"You don't suspect him, then?"

"I don't." The sheriff sighed. "Mebbeso you're right, Greg. I kinda liked the overbearin' bastard, myself. What'd you think of Ric's plan of action? Sounds mightly sensible to me, it does."

"Not to me, sheriff."

"Why not?"

"Sounds kinda childish. Him on a butte back in the badlands spyin' on them Cullens sonsofbitches. You on Flat Top Butte, gettin' instructions he flashes by a hand mirror he packs."

The sheriff nodded, listening.

"Then me or one of my hands on Black Butte watchin' both you an' him an' you—"

"You won't be able to see either him or me," the sheriff said. "The distance is too far for naked eyework."

"I know. Credit me with a nickel's worth of brains, at least. He'll flash a signal to you—then you flash one toward Black Butte—"

"An ol' thing," the sheriff said. "Some claim that the early pioneers traded lookin' glasses to the Injuns jus' so the squaws could look at themselves, but that wasn't the reason."

Mattson killed a horsefly on the roan's off shoulder.

"Injuns used them lookin' glasses to flash messages for miles tellin' the whereabouts of them white-dog soldiers an' things like that."

Another horsefly landed. It died in its tracks, too.

"General Miles telegrammed by mirrors

when he chased Sittin' Bull into Canady after Crazy Horse kilt thet idiot of a Custer."

Mattson's patience had run its length. "Yeah, an' for what it's worth, Miles used lookin' glasses to communicate when he was at the north end of the Bearpaws—south of Chinook—an' when he did Chief Joseph an' the poor tired squaws an' kins came in, remember?"

"Miles is a hell of a good man," the sheriff said. "I sure wish he'd had run for president last election."

"Anythin' would beat what we got in the White House now," Greg Mattson said.

"But I never come here to spiel politics," Sheriff Ratchford informed him. "I rid out here to see if you an' your waddies would help me an' Ric corral them bastardly Cullen's rustlers."

"Right nice thought of you, sheriff."

Sheriff Ike Ratchford scowled. This young man didn't seem to take this seriously. He was up against something he didn't understand and in such cases he became angry—and anger was now rising.

Greg sure t'hell wasn't the fightin' bastard his ol' father had been. Ol' Scott would have headed right out fast after them cowthieves with a six shooter tied onto his hip an' a loaded rifle in his hands, waddies streakin' behin' on tough horses, all of them also loaded with killer hardware!

And on the way to the gunfight ol' Scott might have picked up his ol' trail buddy, Brent Williams, and a handful of Bar Diamond cowpokes an' ol' Brent and his rifles would have ridden with Scott. . . .

In them days, cowpokes were loyal to their irons. They'd die for their brands. But nowadays—

Sheriff Ike Ratchford spat hugely.

What was the world comin' to, anyway?

He opened his mouth to shoot out a hot bunch of words, but Greg Mattson spoke too soon. "Now let's say it's a cloudy day an' no sun—Or dark night an' impossible to reflect light from a mirror—"

"Yeah?"

"Then what do we use for a signal?"

"You read Ric's letter, didn't you?"

"Yeah, he said somethin' about buildin' a small fire in back of where them rustlers is. You'd see this fire on Flat Top Butte an' you'd signal by fire whoever was on Black Butte an' get the word through that way."

"Like the Hunkpapa Sioux usta signal, Greg. Small fire, hold a blanket in front of it—three times blottin' it out, was the rule, An' Ric says that's what he'd do."

"What's to keep them Cullens from seein' the fire?"

"Ric'll be behin' the rustlers—west of 'em—with hill atween him an' them so's they kint see the fire. Hell, that's easy to arrange."

"Okay, I'll post a man on Black Butte. You know, I've done a lot of riding—an' thinkin'—the last few day, 'specially since Ric done hauled ass out."

"Ridin'? An' thinkin'?"

"Yeah, both. Never knew I was capable of thinkin', did you now?"

The lawman grinned. He liked this young guy and at the same time he didn't like him. Life was just a hell of a mess of stupid contradictions.

"We'll let that ride," the sheriff said. "What you been thinkin' about?"

"Well, first I talked to each an' every one of them seven farmers Ric hauled in. I talked civilly an' as a frien', although it was hard to do."

"What'd you talk about?"

"Well, I led up to it gradually. Each could homestead an' I'd pay each twenty bucks a month an' when they had deeds to their homesteads they'd sell each an' every deed to me for a coupla hundred bucks—an' Half Circle V would own their land, then."

"What'd they say?"

"Each an' every manjack of 'em turned me down. I even went to forty bucks per month—with them doin' nothin' but settin'—an' five hundred each deed, an' they still turned me down."

"They must wanta stay, eh?"

"They sure do. So then an' there I come to one conclusion, sher'ff."

"An' thet?"

"No use fightin' them. That'd land some of us dead an' the rest in Uncle Sam's federal pen. Work with them. Buy their hay for stock feed. An' get my cowpokes on homesteads jus' as fas' as Ric can lay them homesteads out!"

Sheriff Ike Ratchford suddenly felt at least eighty years younger. He took out his red bandana and mopped his sweaty forehead. "You showed logic, Greg—real deep logic, man. An' I congratulate you."

"I took you off the fish-hook, eh?"

"Me an' lotsa others, Greg."

"Now let's talk about cows. No, not them rustled cows of mine—jes' cows, plain cows."

"Okay. Shoot."

"These damn', worthless longhorns, fer instance, Ric was wise. He got rid of all of his'n. Shipped 'em out to the last horn. I'm goin' do the same. Pull the last big longhorn roundup, like Ric did."

"An' then what?"

"Stock the ranch with good cattle. Angus, Shorthorns, Herefords. Ain't made up my min' jus' what breed, yet."

"I'd say Herefords were the best. I've read they kin take a awful tough winter an' not much winter-kill."

"I'll run an open range till it's all gone. Then my cowpunchers'll deed grass-homesteads to me. An' the way I figure, some parts of this country—the hills an' rough section—will never be homestead. No farmin' land there."

"I agree."

"Okay, we got that settled. Now, let's talk about them rustlers—an' them cows of mine they been stealin'."

"An' aim to steal at the present time."

"Them original wagons, now. I think they carry butcherin' equipment—tripods folded down, things like thet."

"So Ric's letter said."

"Them water wagons, now. They'll furnish water in the badlands. I only got one big question."

"An' it, son?"

"Let's say the Cullens kill an' butcher back in the badlands. Won't the meat spoil in this heat goin' all the way acrost country to the Little Rockies?"

"I've considered that. Them wagons might have salt sacks."

"I see. They'd salt the meat down good before movin' it, eh?"

"Thet's my opinion," Sheriff Ratchford said.

Mattson rubbed a whiskery jaw. "I agree. But what say we get a signal from Ric sayin' them rustlers are leavin' the badlands?"

"Keep on."

"Ric flashes to Flat Top. Your man there flashes to my man on Black Butte. We head out acrost country for thet canyon the wagons entered. An' by the time we get there them wagons'll be acrost the Milk an' headin' south."

"I've thought of that. Best place we could catch them is in thet narrow canyon."

"You're right, sheriff. So here's what I think we'd best do."

"Shoot, Greg."

"You station somebody on Flat Top. I

put a hand on Black Butte. But you an' me ain't in this locality. We're down on the Milk watchin' thet canyon along with as many men as I kin raise to help us, which I think is damn' few. These new cowpunchers—them new breed—they ain't got much loyalty to the iron thet pays their wages."

"I reckon they don't, Greg. I was thinkin' of the same plan. Come mornin' we head out, headin' for thet canyon."

"I'll meet you in town, sheriff." Mattson patted his horse's shoulders. "Damn thet Ric. A stupid son, thet fool. Ridin' all thet way alone—into thet gunsmoke territory—"

Sheriff Ratchford said nothing.

"Ridin' to see who butchers my cows—an' me not askin' him to. The stupid bastard might've got hisself kilt!"

"Only way peace can come, Greg."

"I meet him, an' you know what I'm goin' do—jus' because he's so damn' bullheaded?"

"What're you goin' do?"

"Beat the crap outa him!"

XIV

But the Cullens did not butcher in the badlands this time. They apparently aimed to butcher somewhere closer to the mountain towns. The reason was simple; terrible summer heat set in. Even though salted down, meat would soon spoil in the torrid climate.

They had a stolen herd of around two hundred Half Circle V cattle waiting, mostly bony steers who were just beginning to put on a little meat, for the grass had grown since the long rain.

From his high vantage point on a tall butte a mile west of the holding-grounds Ric Williams squatted and watched through his field-glasses, his horse hidden behind him in the brush.

It was not the best look-out in the world, but the best he could find in this eroded, color-slashed worthless badlands. It had no water for him or his horse.

The butte's flat top held a little soapweed and buck brush, which was very little for a horse to graze on. Actually the bronc wouldn't eat the gray soapweed that clung to the barren earth. Were he to eat this his tail would be up and he'd be physically sick until his belly rumbled.

And Ric depended on a fast and tough horse in good physical shape. He figured the water in his canteen—if used sparingly—would keep him and the horse for two full days, maybe three.

Then he and the bronc would have to go out for water. He figured the closest water lay straight east out of the badlands at Carson's Well, a natural always-flowing spring on what had been the boundary between his father's Bar Diamond Bar and Scott Mattson's Half Circle V.

From where he hunkered he could see Flat Top Butte some ten miles to the east, an upthrust heaved by nature millions of years ago into the blue Montana sky.

He could not see Black Butte. Distance hid the black-topped dome.

He tried out the little hand-mirror he always carried in his saddle-bag the morning of the second day. The sun was rising and he was sure the reflection could be seen on tall Flat Top.

He pointed the mirror toward the sun.

He moved it in short, jerky motions. He then waited. He got no returning flash. He tried again; again, he drew a blank.

It then occurred to him that the sun was behind whoever was on Flat Top—if, indeed anybody were there. Thus the person there could not flash a signal toward the west but only to the east and partways north and south.

This signal idea—by mirrors—wasn't so efficient. . . .

He tried again when the sun was at noon. He again got no reply. Another try, then another—still, no answer. Doubt struck him. Had young Hoffard delivered his message to Sheriff Ike Ratchford?

His spirits suddenly lifted. For far to the east, from the rocky summit on Flat Top, came a series of flashes, plainly the reflection of a mirror.

He had seen the Great Northern's telegraph operators down in Malta click out the Morse Code but of course he knew nothing about transmitting the code. He'd explained this in his letter to Sheriff Ratchford.

Four flashes would indicate that the cattle were being moved. On the last flash he would twist his mirror as much as possible to show the direction the stolen steers were headed.

If he signaled by fire, three interruptions would mean the cattle were being butchered on the spot, four that they were being moved south. He now wished he'd made a similar arrangement regarding the mirror-flashes but he hadn't and it was too late now.

Elation touched him. His message had got through to the lawman. He felt sure Sheriff Ratchford would notify Greg Mattson.

Those steers—those stolen steers—below bore Mattson's brand, so surely Mattson would be concerned? Ric Williams a few times had mentally kicked himself in the rump for trailing down these rustlers. These cows were not his. And he faced the simple truth: this might end in a gun-battle.

And a bullet didn't give a hoot in hell who it killed.

Still, this rustling had to be halted, for once and for all. Black Butte range had to have peace. For without peace and lawfulness, there could be no progress.

And progress, to Ric Williams, meant nice farm homes, schools, churches, and happy families.

He was sure Greg Mattson and Sheriff Ratchford would have others helping them. He'd asked the sheriff to intercept the wagons when they came out of the badlands ten or so miles south, just north of Milk River.

He soon saw how the cow-thieves operated. Moonlight was bright and they gathered from the cattle wandering close to the east edge of the worthless country.

These were chased into the labryinthine area some five miles and at this point they were held in a rather large natural clearing, the floor of which was alkali soil and soapweeds.

Here the cattle had been butchered. Ric's field-glasses showed wooden tripods dismantled and lying on the side of a hill. He saw newly-disturbed earth at the base of the north hill.

He guessed hides and guts and heads and hoofs were buried there. Thus no stink could waft eastward and hit the nostrils of cowpunchers riding the edge of the rough country.

The thieves had even hauled in a wooden water tank. This they filled with water from water wagons. Ric was not surprised when bales of hay were pulled out of the tarp-covered wagons and distributed around the hungry cattle.

He was not surprised when he saw no cattle being butchered. He'd half-expected the gang to drive the stock out and butcher somewhere closer to the mountains because of the terrible heat.

He felt sure these rustlers had operated some time back in this god-forsaken area of salt grass and alkali. No cowpuncher would ride this deep into the badlands. Even the most stupid would know no cow would wander this far into this hell.

He counted the cow-thieves. First, the three Cullens, killers all. Then seven skinners on the wagons; two on the water-wagons. That made twelve. Then three cow-punchers had been here when the wagons had rolled in.

These three had been slyly hazing Half Circle V cattle into the edges of the badlands. Now that the wagons had arrived they began shoving these cattle toward the Cullen camping-area.

Ric had lots of time to think. And most of the time, his thoughts went toward women, centering on dark-haired Martha Stewart, then on light-haired Jennie

Queen—but mostly settled on thin waisted Melissa Wentworth.

Yes, and he thought of Kid Hannigan, too.

First, why would a man Hannigan's age, and stocky, bearded build be called the *Kid?* Hannigan certainly was beyond the boyhood age. He dismissed this thought as irrelevant.

But what had called Kid Hannigan to the Little Rocky Mountains? What earthly reason had the Kid to be in that gold-mad town? Had he quit Greg Mattson? And had he ridden south?

Where was Hannigan now?

At that moment Kid Hannigan was in Sheriff Ike Ratchford's office in Black Butte. Greg Mattson was also there, slouched in a chair, cold cigarette hanging from his bottom lip.

"Never learned a damn' thing in them mountains," Hannigan was saying. "There's a lot of meat comin' in there from somewhere but damn' if I could fin' out where it's comin' from." He looked at Greg Mattson. "Might jus' as well come out with it, Mattson. The Association sent me here to stop this rustlin'—but I ain't got off homeplate in my investigation."

"Kinda figured that," Greg Mattson said.

"Why didn't you tell us?" the sheriff asked.

"My orders was to work without nobody knowin' my real chore. I've worked for the Association for years now on a number of jobs but this is the first one that's stumped me."

"It didn't stump Ric Williams," Ratchford pointed out.

Hannigan looked at the lawman. "What'd you mean by that, sheriff?"

Sheriff Ratchford told him. Hannigan listened and his forehead was grooved. His brows rose at the mention of Ric spotting him in the mountain gold-camp.

"Hell, I never seen him." the detective said.

"He saw you," the sheriff said.

Hannigan asked, "What plan of procedure are we goin' use, sheriff?"

"You ridin' out with us?" Greg Mattson asked.

Hannigan spread his hands significantly. "I'm a stock detective. My orders are to see that every job I'm on is brought to a successful conclusion. This one so far ain't been done so. It's my job to see that it is."

Sheriff Ratchford shifted in his swivel chair. "Here's our deal, detective. Greg an' me has looked it over from all angles an' come to a conclusion."

Kid Hannigan nodded.

"Ric's flashed out there's fifteen cow-thieves. He's given out that many flashes at once, a signal he mentioned in his letter. They'll head out south on the road they entered the badlands on—north of the Milk at Squaw Crossin'."

"Don't know were Squaw Crossin' is," Hannigan said.h

"A few miles west of Willow Point," the sheriff explained, and lifted a hand to still keep the floor. "You won't know where thet is, either—but it makes no never-mind."

"Seein' it makes no never-mind, then howcome you mention it?" Kid Hannigan asked.

"Jus' in passin'," the sheriff explained. "Willow Point is the west limit of the sheriff down in Malta. My county dips down to the Milk there so Squaw Crossin' is under my jurisdiction—and my sworn duty says I'm to enforce the law impartially an' completely throughout my entire county."

"Well said," Hannigan assured. "What'd we do, then?"

Greg Mattson spoke for the first time in a long time. "We get our hands down on the Milk in the timber where their trail comes out. An' we stop them then an' there, Hannigan."

"How many hands we got, boss?"

Greg lit a cigarette. "There's the sheriff, an' me, an' you—an' only three others."

"Who are they?" Hannigan asked.

"Old hands thet came up with my father and mother an' the longhorns years ago from Texas. I asked my other hands if they'd fight for the range ag'in rustlers if the rustlers could be found."

"What'd they say?"

"Under no circumstances."

Kid Hannigan scowled. "The new-fangled breed of cowpokes," he told the world. "What'd you then do, boss?"

"I fired the whole goddamned bunch. I'm hirin' new hands after this is settled and—" He told of the oncoming roundup to clean his range of longhorns. "So that's the deal, Hannigan."

Hannigan rubbed his whiskers. "We'll be outnumbered by a few guns. How we gonna fight them?"

Greg Mattson spoke to Sheriff Ratchford. "You tell him, sheriff. You thought of the idea."

Sheriff Ike Ratchford carefully and fully explained.

XV

THE DAY was terribly hot with a cloudless sky until five in the afternoon when dark clouds came up out of the northwest.

Ric had doled out his last spoonful of water to his saddle-horse at noon that day. He and his horse had to go out for water or perish.

He could not go east to water at Carson's Well. To reach the Well he'd have to pass through enemy lines. And if seen —Gunfire, immediately. And the odds were too great for one man alone. . . .

The rustlers had done no butchering. Plainly they intended to drive the herd out and butcher somewhere else. Both water-tanks were empty. He'd seen the last of the water pulled out of each that afternoon.

The rustlers were without hay, too. Cattle bawled weakly against thirst and hunger.

The cows had not eaten the last of the hay. They now trampled it under hoofs. They were too thirsty to eat. Common sense told Ric the cattle would have to soon be moved to water.

Darkness finally came. The sun tipped down into the west. Overhead the clouds were darker.

Ric figured the clouds were filled with rain. When darkness was complete he built a small fire back on the butte where it could not be seen from below.

He took off his shirt. He made three deliberate passes with his shirt in front of the fire, the agreed signal saying the herd was being moved. He got no answering flashes from Flat Top.

He tried two times. Still, no answering signals. There was nothing he could do but leave.

The dry taste of defeat was sour in his mouth. Nobody had been on Flat Top. He put his mind to work and in this thinking received new hope.

Sheriff Ike Ratchford was an old and experienced hand at this law-enforcement business. He'd not be in Black Butte town or on Black Butte. He'd be with his posse south along Milk River waiting either for a herd of stolen cattle or wagons of butchered but stolen beef to come out of the rough country, heading south toward the Little Rocky Mountains.

But still, it seemed logical he should have somebody stationed on Flat Top Butte to give a return signal, wasn't it? Or was it?

Ric's plan was to water himself and his horse in Milk River. Then if the sheriff and Greg Mattson were not in the cottonwoods there he'd bird-dog the rustled cattle to their butchering spot, and thus know where they'd been slaughtered, at least.

Rain hit him on the back a few miles from his hiding place. It came in with a strong wind. He was wet before he could untie his black oilskin slicker from the back of his saddle, so he rode on without the raincoat's protection.

The cloudburst whipped in with driving rains. Within a few minutes water careened off the sidehills, dirty and fast-flowing. The water question was rapidly solved.

The horse drank from mudholes. Ric washed his face and cupped dirty water to his lips.

Then he rode on.

The cloudburst stopped as suddenly as it had begun. The badlands were soaked. The wagon-road was slippery slime. The moon wheeled upright, round and big and yellow. Moonlight glistened off pools of water.

There now was no wind. The world was clean and golden, the rough hills standing out in clear relief. He rode out of the badlands onto the level land leading south to Milk River.

Small coulees carried run-off water into the river. Ric rode through the darkness of the cottonwood trees. He'd cross the river and ride across the south prairie to hide in the southern hills until the herd and the wagons and the rustlers emerged.

He came to the river. Here was a rocky crossing with a hard bottom and water about hub-deep on a farm wagon. His horse demanded more water. Ric let the bronc lower his head and drink.

He looked about, a feeling of tension running across his belly. Moonlight glistened on the rushing water, now muddy from the rain. Finally, the horse had drunk his fill. He raised his head.

Then it was that a harsh voice behind him said, "Up with them han's, fella! Move quick, damn' it!"

Ric raised his hands, reins around the saddle-horn. He immediately recognized the stern voice.

"Ike Ratchford," he said.

There was a moment's pause. Then the voice said, "By golly, if it ain't Ric Williams! Couldn't recognize you right off in them shadows, nor your cayuse either."

Ric lowered his hands. "Figured you might be here, sheriff. Who you got with you?"

"Boys are back in the brush, waitin'. This way, Ric boy. Good to see you again, son."

"Glad to be here," Ric said, grinning crookedly.

That was the understatement of his short lifetime. Behind him came a herd of rustled cattle—now about three hundred head, he guessed—and behind that came the wagons. And all reported one thing—red, roaring, flaming guns. For these rustlers wouldn't give in without gunsmoke, Ric knew.

For more than stolen cattle was at stake. The very lives of the three Cullen brothers —Clyde, Ed and Lon—were in danger. For if captured alive, there was only one thing ahead for each and every one of these thieves —and that was the hangman's noose. . . .

For if captured these men would never see the inside of a court-room. They would be hanged immediately and on the spot.

A catch-rope, tossed up over a sturdy cottonwood branch, the noose around the rustler's neck as he sat his horse under the branch, hands tied behind his back.

The rope's other end anchored to another tree. Then the horse the rustler bestrode hammered over the rump with a doubled-catch-rope.

The horse leaping ahead. The rustler sliding back from the saddle, then hitting the end of the rope—boots a foot off the ground, the fall breaking his neck and killing him immediately.

Then, a shallow grave, back in the timber. Maybe a cross over it made of wood, maybe nothing. A grave that in time would level with the other ground through howling blizzards and roaring cloudbursts.

Each of the Cullens—and the men with them—knew their fate if captured, and Ric Williams was damned sure they'd fight until death.

He followed Sheriff Ike Ratchford into the brush, the sheriff explaining that he'd left a man on Flat Top Butte, but the bastard might have gone to sleep. They came to a clearing. Here were saddled horses. Ric counted eight. He remembered there were fifteen rustlers.

Odds always favored the bunch with the most gun. Thus the odds favored the fighting Cullen brothers and their twelve gunhands.

The posse hunkered back into the darkness. One voice said, "Good to see you again, Ric."

"Same to you, Kid Hannigan."

"They say you saw me in the mountains. I'm an Association detective, an' I travel under cover. You found the rustlers, though, an' not me—so how about me recommendin' you to the Association as a detective?"

Ric grinned, "We'll discuss that later, Hannigan."

"Yeah," the detective said, "later. . . ."

Ric knew what Hannigan meant. There might not be a *later* for some of these men, including one Ric Williams.

Another voice said, "Howdy, Ric."

"Howdy, Gus."

"Good to see you, Ric," another voice said from the darkness.

"Same here to you, Stan."

An old voice creaking with age, said, "Men sometimes meet under strange circumstances, Ric."

"Right you are, Lee."

Lee Porter, Stan Musket and Gus Welton were long-time Half Circle V hands who trailed up from the Lone Star state with Scott Mattson and Brent Williams. To them the only home they ever had was the roof provided for them by the Mattson family.

All were well into their sixties, Ric knew —possibly Lee was in his early seventies. His heart fell. He had a weak fighting force on his side. He then realized one had not greeted him.

This man stood well back into the shadows. Ric saw he was big and tall and he guessed he was Gregory Mattson but he wasn't sure until he heard Greg say, "Well, here we are, Williams."

His voice still held his old cynicism. Once again it grated on Ric Williams, rising his blood a degree or two. Wasn't the man even going to thank him for risking his neck in finding these rustlers?

"How are you, Greg?"

"Waitin'," Greg Mattson said.

The tension was so thick you could cut it with a dull Bowie knife. Ric was aware of it and he knew all the others had to be, also. He was glad when the sheriff said, "All right, Ric, tell us what you know."

Ric talked rapidly, explained, then said, "What's your plan of action, sheriff?"

Sheriff Ratchford told him. Ric listened carefully, all the time smelling kerosene—and why kerosene out in this wilderness?

He soon discovered the answer.

XVI

GUN-HUNG AND all killer, Clyde Cullen rode point, Winchester .40-.40 crossed in front of his amarillo saddle, his blue roan strong and tough under the saddle.

The roan's flanks were full. He'd watered from run-off water back in the hills. He was fresh and wanted the trails, pulling on the reins.

Behind Clyde Cullen came three hundred and twenty-four head of stolen Half Circle V longhorns, spooky and edgy, swinging their razor tipped racks, ready to fight man or beast.

Cloven hoofs ground Montana mud. Where but a few moments before had been liquid dust was now sloppy mud. Steers slipped, fell. Others walked over them, horns down, looking for trouble.

Behind the herd rode five riders, including the two other Cullen outlaws—morose Lon and grim-faced Ed. These riders hazed the cattle forward. They were soaked to the bone and wet and angry but each had been sure to cover his pouched pistol with a bandana or such when the cloudburst had hit.

A man never knew. . . . Even if powder were encased in a waterproof brass cap was no sure sign that the powder would be kept dry during a rain. A man had best take precautions. Cover your pistol with your bandana or better yet take it from your holster and push it down inside your belt in front under your shirt.

Behind the hazers came the nine wagons, the empty water wagons taking up the rear, the seven farm wagons directly behind the hazers. Broad rimmed wheels slipped in mud. Shod work-horses had rough walking on the white alkali spots. These were very slippery. Water had penetrated the white alkali but a few inches making it sloppy as soup.

The cattle had drunk their fill from mudholes along the way. They now wanted to get on grass; still, few did any bawling. They moved south—a sea of glistening horns, an ocean of broad wet backs—headed for Milk River and the grass of the open prairie.

They moved in almost silence. The whole thing had a ghostly air about it. The tall, bony man riding point, Winchester at the ready, a killer and highway-robber wanted in many states throughout the West.

And behind him the stolen cattle, moving silently forward, compact and powerful—ready to explode into violent, murderous action for the slightest reason.

And overhead the cloudless night sky of old Montana. The blue, endless sky that now held a full moon which threw brilliant light over the badlands, the wagons, the hazers, the herd and the stern killer who rode gun-guard in the front, Clyde Allen Cullen.

Clyde Cullen rode a hundred feet ahead of the horns behind him. When he came out of the badlands he was clearly seen under the moonlight. He drew rein for a long moment, Winchester half raised, and he rose slightly on stirrups, eyes moving here, then there searching and probing—a wolf in saddle, a lobo sniffing the air, searching out trouble before trouble searched him out.

The slight wind was from the southwest. It brought him a strange scent, an odor which definitely should not be present in this wilderness air. Was it the faint smell of kerosene?

Eyes missing nothing, hard fingers curled around the rifle's stock just behind the trigger, he considered this point—and sniffled again, deeper this time. He held the air in his lungs, examining it; finally, he exhaled, deciding his nose had played false.

He looked at the dark rim of timber almost a quarter mile away that rimmed Milk River. He swept his eyes along it. He saw nothing alien and the moonlight was bright and clear.

He settled back in saddle. His fingers lost some of their firmness on the rifle's stock. All was well. This herd would soon be across the river and threading its way south through the hills toward the butchering-spot. All was okay.

He twisted on oxbow stirrups. He looked behind him. The cattle were leaving the ravine. They rolled south in dark silence. He glimpsed his brother Ed, riding right flank. Lon would have haze left flank. And behind would lumber the nine wagons.

He raised his right arm. The signal meant all was well and to push cows ahead. Then he straightened in saddle and gigged his roan ahead—into the raw flames of roaring hell!

For suddenly a hundred feet ahead flame

lanced upward into the moonlight. He pulled in savagely, horse rearing, his rifle at the ready, wondering first if an errant lightning bolt had not hit the prairie ahead, driving even the wet earth into snarling redness.

He then quickly noticed that three fires had been started and when each had whipped both directions. He remembered the acrid smell of kerosene. His quick mind rapidly drew conclusions.

Somebody had spread something dry—like old hay—in a half-circle ahead, had soaked this with kerosene and had just now lit it afire. One match had started the fire in the middle, directly ahead. Two other matches had ignited this kerosene-barrier on each corner where the hills came down and formed a natural funnel.

The terrible truth hit him, driving red across his brain. He and his brothers had ridden into a gun-trap!

For one blinding red second, the world stood still. Here was this outlaw risen on stirrups, frozen in saddle, rifle half raised, stern eyes trying to pierce this rising ring of fire—and seeing nothing through the flames.

And the longhorns behind . . . They, too, were a solid, ugly mass, eyes wide and reflecting fire, horns down and ready to charge to kill—but yet knowing they, like all bovines, would never, never rush through fire.

And behind them the hazers, also high on stirrups, trying to stare over the backs of the cattle, wondering just what the hell was going on out there on the prairie.

And behind the hazers the nine strung-out wagons in the narrow badland defile, halted now with rearing, plunging horses smashing against collars, horses that wanted to run ahead into what they figured was freedom—hazers and drivers and wagons and teams penned behind thousands of pounds of longhorn power that might, at any moment, bolt backwards.

Lon Cullen spurred ahead, smashing his big sorrel stud through the cattle fighting to reach his brother's side up there ahead, just inside this ring of roaring fire.

Back of him rode Ed Cullen, spurs working, catch-rope smashing cattle left and right, short-gun tied to his hip, rifle still in boot but loaded and needing only slithering from leather case.

Then, the cattle wheeled, and stampeded.

There was a grand mixup of mad cattle and mad men on horseback. Two rustlers went down, hoofs grinding over them and their fallen horses. Somehow Ed and Lon

Cullen made it through, a steer ripping the entrails from Lon's horse, sending the horse lunging forward, guts trailing, to collapse and die, kicking angrily and without gain against death.

"Kill the sonsofbitches!" roared Clyde Cullen.

Lon Cullen screamed, "I'm on foot, brother!"

Clyde Cullen reined his roan close. "Swing on behin' me!"

Their only hope was to drive horses through the flames. All knew that a horse is scared to death of fire and many times has to be blindfolded to be led from a burning barn but also knew that if driven hard by spur and whip a horse will, if forced, dash through fire.

For there was no retreat. The canyon behind was a grinding, deadly melee of struggling, striving cattle, of cowboys dehorsed and being ground down, of wagons with teams gutted by horns—the entire defile a clogged, striving, deadly area of combat of man against animal, and with the animal sure to win because of sheer power.

Never before had Ric Williams seen such a scene. Gus Welton had torched the center of the dry hay that had come from an old haystack a rancher had built of hay cut on the river's north side.

Stan Musket had lit fire to the west end, Lee Porter firing the east. The three old timers had all lit their sulphurs at the correct moment. They'd then run into cover back along the river in the brush.

For Ric had said stoutly that none of the old-timers would face the rifles and short-guns of the Cullen gang. This left Sheriff Ratchford, Kid Hannigan, Greg Mattson and Ric against the three Cullen gang.

Kid Hannigan was put out of business within a few seconds. A Cullen bullet dropped the detective's horse. The horse fell on his right side. He imprisoned Hannigan's leg under him and pinned the man down.

Hannigan's rifle slid from his grasp. It landed out of reach. He reached for his pistol. It, too, had fallen. It also could not be reached by the pinned-down, angry man.

"Take the bastard the nearest to you!" Sheriff Ratchford spurred toward Clyde Cullen, six-shooter pounding lead into the moonlight.

From the corner of his eye, Ric saw Clyde Cullen fall from saddle, with Sheriff

Ratchford plunging on, riding hard with six-shooter upraised.

Greg Mattson screamed. "The one over west for me!" He meant Ed Cullen, and his six-gun also flamed—the gun of Ed Cullen also red and ugly.

The two—Mattson and Cullen—rode toward each other. Then, Ed Cullen slid from the saddle, horse loping on, and Mattson pulled in, bronc rearing.

That left Lon Cullen for Ric. Cullen left saddle, landed on one knee, rifle raised—and he shot once. Ric never knew where the bullet went but it missed.

He roared past the kneeling outlaw. And, as he went by Cullen, he leaned low in stirrup, using his .45 as a club—and he smashed steel across the outlaw's skull as Cullen fought feverishly to jack a fresh cartridge into his rifle's barrel.

Lon Cullen went down on his face in the mud, knocked cold. Ric wheeled his horse and stared about, six-shooter ready—but this part of the fighting was over.

The three old timers ran from the timber. Back in the canyon cattle bawled as they smashed over horses and wagons. Within a few minutes, the only living member of the Cullen gang, Lon Cullen, joined his brothers in death—he being on the end of a hangman's rope.

When Kid Hannigan had been freed from under his dead horse he'd grinned and said, "Hell of a detective I make. Even my hoss has got it in for me, him pinnin' me down like thet. I owe my life to you, sheriff. An' to you two, too. Mattson an' Williams."

A stray bullet had caught Greg Mattson high on the left arm. He held a bloody bandana over the wound. "No, don't need your help, Williams," he said shortly. "I'll get along without your sidin' me."

Ric bit off a hot reply.

"Ain't got no bones broken." Mattson said. "Jus' a bullet through the meat, no more—thank God fer thet."

The sheriff spoke to Gus Welton. "You an' Greg head down river to Malta an' the doctor."

"Jus' as you say, sher'ff."

Mattson's horse was fidgety. Mattson got his left boot in stirrup, grabbed for the horn with his good hand, missed. Ric stepped forward, plainly aiming to help.

"I don't need your help, Williams. God damn it, can't you understan' the King's English!"

Ric stepped back. He glanced at the

sheriff. Ratchford had a long, sour face. He didn't meet Ric's gaze.

Ric then knew he and Greg Mattson would be enemies until one of them died. It wasn't a good thought, but it was reality. And it had no reason for being, but it was there—and apparently always would be there.

Mattson got into leather. He and Gus Welton rode south and out of sight.

Sheriff Ratchford said, "We'll have to bury this man. Damned if I'd know where a shovel is. Guess we'll have to get one outa Malta."

"I'll ride in with Greg an' Gus an' bring one out," old timer Stan Musket said.

Soon he too loped east.

Ric said, "I reckon we'd best go up the canyon an' see if anybody's livin' after them dogies got done with those wagons an' teams an' drivers."

He still felt heavy at heart because of Greg Mattson's rebuffs.

The four of them walked into the canyon's black mouth with rifles at the ready, a needless precaution, for they met no gunfire. Everywhere was bleak and bloody destruction.

Cattle were down, some dead, some

living. Two gutted broncs lay still harnessed next to destroyed wagons. Rifles and six-guns soon put the injured animals out of business.

Twelve men had been behind the herd. Five lay dead, hoof-hammered to the mud. The other seven apparently had escaped by somehow climbing the canyon's steep and slippery walls.

"They'll never return to rustle another cow," Kid Hannigan said. "Bet wherever they are they're still runnin'."

"No use tryin' to trail 'em." the sheriff said. "Man might ride into an ambush an' be kilt. We've been damn' lucky so far in this. Lots more luck than I figured on."

"That's no understatement," old Lee Porter said.

They tied the dead men together at the ankles and pulled them out through the mud to where lay the three dead Cullens, using a catch-rope Lee Porter came back with after taking it from the saddle of dead Lon Cullen.

"I'm leavin' in the mornin'," Kid Hannigan told them. "If I went back to Black Butte, thet farmer Jim Young'd sure as heck pick trouble with me. He bumped me that day of the stampede on purpose. He seems to hate the very sight of me an' don't ask me why. Some men jus' seem born to hate the other man, I reckon."

"There's truth in thet," Sheriff Ratchford said.